Child of the Red Land

Cécile Drouin was born in 1938 in Hanoi, where her father was director of the Indochina Water and Power Company. At the end of 1945 the family moved to France. Cécile Drouin became a freelance journalist, publishing articles from Israel, Vietnam (where she covered the war for *Newsweek* and other periodicals) and the Seychelles, as well as throughout France. She is the author of two books of popular child psychology; *Child of the Red Land* is her first novel.

After working for many years, Jan Dalley is now a freelance editor, translator and reviewer who writes for the *Observer* and *Times Literary Supplement*, among other publications. Her previous published translations include an illustrated edition of *Pushkin's Fairy Tales*.

GW00362758

Cécile Drouin

Child of the
Red Land

Translated from the French by Jan Dalley

Pan Books
in association with Chatto & Windus

First published in Great Britain 1988 by
Chatto & Windus Ltd
This edition published 1989 by Pan Books Ltd,

Cavaye Place, London SW10 9PG
in association with Chatto & Windus Ltd

9 8 7 6 5 4 3 2 1

© Editions Sylvie Messinger 1985
Translation © Chatto & Windus Ltd 1988

ISBN 0 330 30542 5

Printed and bound in Great Britain by
Cox & Wyman Ltd, Reading

For Thi Ba,
For the Thâns, so that they will protect me,
For that Strasbourg soldier,
For Leonard Cohen, whom I don't know
    but who makes me dream,
For Christian and Sylvie, without whom
    this book would not exist.

CHAPTER ONE

The white bars are broken on one side.

When I was little I always wanted to get out of bed, but I couldn't. I just lay there, feeling bored. I used to slip one foot through the bars, or one hand.

Once I managed to get my head through.

I was stuck. The bars wouldn't let me go.

It hurt. I didn't dare cry out. Anyway, who would have heard me? My room was all by itself at the top of the house. I waited. I waited for as long as it was dark outside.

There were some Japanese soldiers on the balcony. They were asleep. Or perhaps they were pretending, like me.

It was hot and my head stuck to the bars. I tried not to go to sleep so that they wouldn't come and kill me while I was a prisoner. It seemed a long time. Everything always seems a long time, except when you're eating. Then it's over very quickly.

When it got light Thi Ba came in. She let out a great scream, as loud as people do when you kill them. She ran out of the room, as if she was abandoning me.

I waited a bit longer, and Daddy came. It was the first time he'd ever been into my room. Daddy is always with other people. He was very angry. He scolded me. Then he broke the bars and made a gap.

I'm bigger now. I'm five years old. I can get out of bed by myself, although I'm too wide to get through the gap. I stand up, bend my knees, and jump. Not just anywhere, though. You have to be careful. There is a big stain on the floor and if I step on it it will bring me bad luck. Thi Ba

7

told me. It's because the stain looks like a dragon, and you must never step on a dragon. If you do it doesn't like it and it gets angry.

Thi Ba is very scared of dragons. She's even afraid of the kind you can eat, which are ordinary animals. When the bep catches one she starts to cry. She runs away so she can't see it.

The bep found one today. It was as thick as my leg. He put it on the kitchen table. He took the chopper and cut the dragon into slices. There was blood all over the table. All over the floor, too. The dragon was fighting and trying to run away, but the bep held it very tight and it couldn't. When you can't run away you just have to die.

The other beps eat dragons. It makes them strong and brave. But our bep has a blackbird that sings. It has to be fed with little bits of dragon, otherwise it won't sing any more. Because of that we never eat dragons in our house. Since the bep does the cooking, he decides what we have to eat.

Anyway, Thi Ba wouldn't eat a dragon. She'd be too frightened. She's always scared of everything. But if she did eat a bit she wouldn't be afraid of them any more. You can't be afraid of the people you eat.

More than anything, Thi Ba is scared of the spirit dragons. The biggest is the Holy Dragon. His heart is in Hue and his body stretches everywhere. To Cochin China and to Tonkin. He's here in Hanoi, too. Under the garden. Sometimes when somebody digs in the garden to plant something to eat, they hurt him. He gets angry and shakes himself. Everything moves and houses fall down.

People die in the houses.

Once upon a time there was a general called Cao-Bien who took some thunder to scare away his enemies. The thunder fell on the dragon, who bled a lot, and the river ran red.

What I'm scared of is the Makouis. They are invisible and very mean. They're always trying to hurt someone.

When you go to bed you must always look underneath it to make sure there isn't a Makoui waiting for you to go to sleep so he can harm you. Usually you look and you don't see anything, but sometimes the Makouis make themselves invisible. They pretend to be human beings. They can turn themselves into Japanese soldiers, for example.

Luckily the Thâns are good, and more powerful too. If someone is protected by the Thâns, the Makouis can't do anything to them.

Every night before I go to sleep I pray to the Thâns. I ask them to look after me and Thi Ba. If I'm feeling brave I talk to them about Mummy and Daddy too. Sometimes I even pretend that I like Natalie.

If I pray badly I have nightmares.

Last night I prayed badly. I was thinking of the tiger Thi Ba told me about.

It was a very old tiger. He had broken teeth and sore paws, so he couldn't run fast enough to catch animals any more. He had to eat people instead.

Thi Ba says this made him unhappy, because the tiger is a lord and man is too easy a prey. It was sad for the people, too. They couldn't go to Nirvana. When you've been eaten by a lord, you aren't allowed to go. You become a ghost until the lord himself dies.

But this old tiger lived on and on. He got older and older and he went on eating people. The ghosts had to ride on his back.

There were lots of them, piled on top of each other. It was exhausting. They quarrelled all the time.

9

There was a very fat and dirty bâ-gia. She was really old and she took up too much space. Nobody liked her. There was also a horrible water-seller. He wanted the best place on the tiger's back, where he could hold on tightly.

Sometimes the ghosts fought, and if they lost they fell off. Then they had to run along behind and climb back up without any help from the others.

In the end there was no more space at all, but the tiger was hungry. He ate a grocer called Caï.

Poor Caï became a very tired ghost. He had to run behind the tiger the whole time because there was no more room on top. The other ghosts teased him, shouting 'Faster, faster' and laughing and pointing at him.

Finally the grocer tried to hang on to the tiger's tail. It was very difficult. Old Caï had no strength left, and he often fell off and hurt himself, so he ran away and went to find his brother.

'Brother Quir,' he pleaded, 'please save me.'

His brother was very surprised. It was night-time, and he had been asleep. At first he thought he was dreaming.

Quir wasn't a believer, and he didn't believe in ghosts. But when he saw that Caï was crying he began to believe.

'How can I save you?' he asked.

'Burn some incense in front of the buddha Cakya Mouni, and say a prayer for me. Then dig a big hole at the entrance to the village, get a baby goat and tether it at the bottom of the pit. Tomorrow, gather all the men in the village together and capture the lord.'

'But brother Caï, isn't it blasphemy to attack a lord?'

'This one has lived long enough.'

The next day, all the ghosts goaded the tiger, scratching and kicking him. Caï pulled his tail to left and right, and they managed to bring him to the village. When the tiger heard the bleating of the kid, he was so hungry that he jumped straight into the pit. The men came running with their choppers and the lord was dead.

The souls all flew away. They were in such a hurry that the old bâ-gia lost her wig and Caï had two teeth torn out.

Thi Ba says this is a true story.

I'm hot. The fan in my bedroom is broken. It has been broken for a long time. Nobody has come to fix it. Daddy says it's impossible to find workmen nowadays. I'm not sure if he's right. He's so strange. Yesterday he asked, 'How old is Laurence?' I wonder what would happen if Daddy forgot that I exist. He'd probably be glad.

Mummy and Daddy wanted a Ludovic. That's why they never want to play with me.

It's terrible, not being a Ludovic. It's a mean trick the Makouis played. Thi Ba, who knows everything, explained to me that when Mummy got pregnant (that's an illness a man gives to his wife, and later when the lady has been very ill she has a baby) she didn't want to be so ill again. She had had Natalie and that was enough for her. So Mummy decided to kill me. She called a witch to get the special medicines. Then a man all in black came to the house, wearing a long dress like a lady. He was a sort of magician too, but for white magic. This gentleman had discovered what Mummy wanted to do and he didn't agree. He made a lot of fuss because white magicians never want you to kill babies, even if they are extra babies that nobody wants. What can you do with babies like that?

The magician made such a fuss that Mummy agreed not to kill me on condition that I was a Ludovic. She made a bargain with the magician. Every day she went to pray at a secret place where the white magicians work.

The magician didn't keep his promise: I'm not a Ludovic.

By the time they knew, it was too late to kill me. Mummy wasn't allowed to any more; they would have put her in prison.

Mummy was very angry. She said she'd never pray again, and she wouldn't look after me either. Daddy had to pay Thi Ba to take her place. It's a nuisance, because I always have to be very good so that she can forget I exist, otherwise she might want to kill me again.

I often wonder if the people I meet hold it against me that I'm not a Ludovic, and if they want to kill me too.

Thi Ba says no, because I'm a pretty little Laurence and I might come in useful one day.

I don't want to die. There are often dead people in the street. They look ugly, with deep red holes in them that overflow and make big red stains everywhere. Sometimes they are even in pieces. From time to time I check to see whether I've got a hole in me, or a piece missing. So far, I'm okay.

But I take all the necessary precautions. If you're not really careful, you die as if you were nothing. Without even noticing. And then it's too late.

First of all, you must never bother anyone. As soon as you bother people, they kill you. I have to be extra careful, because Thi Ba can only look after me during the day. At night she's at the other end of the garden, in the servants' quarters.

Often there are two Japanese soldiers on my balcony at night. They are very dangerous and you must always pretend to smile at them. Daddy and Mummy are with Natalie on the first floor and my bedroom and I are all alone on the second. If the Japanese attacked me no one would hear. Not even if I shouted very loud. In any case, Daddy and

Mummy and Natalie wouldn't come to help me, so it's all the same really.

Sometimes at night there are barefoot, silent thieves who slide into rich houses to look for whatever they can get. We used to be a rich house, but they've already taken everything that's easy to carry. The other night one of them slipped in through the window of my bedroom while the Japanese were somewhere else. I immediately pretended to be dead; that way he wouldn't need to kill me, since it had already been done. I stayed completely rigid in my bed, without moving, trying to breathe as little as possible. Luckily he didn't come close, otherwise he would have seen I didn't have a red hole in me and I wasn't in pieces either.

He opened the cupboards, took some of my clothes and then went away again. I told Thi Ba all about it and she said I'd done exactly the right thing.

Thi Ba says it's always stupid to get yourself killed. You should run away first. Living is too much fun. What's more, you can never be sure of going to Nirvana. That's why I'm so careful. Thi Ba says that apart from her and the old bep I shouldn't trust anyone. White people especially. If one day a bomb falls on the house without killing me then I must run away as far as possible and try to find a yellow family who will have me. Otherwise, I'll fall into the hands of the white wizards. They're always ready to pick up little children who have no one left, but they make them work so hard they get ill. Little girls like me are made to embroider all day long, and even all night, and by the time they're old enough to get married they are almost blind. What's worse, the white wizards make you pray to white gods who bring unhappiness.

But since the white wizards are very powerful, it's difficult for a yellow person to find work without them. So someone

13

in each family has to sacrifice themselves and belong to the god of the white wizards. Then they give him work and he can get enough for all his family to eat.

Finding things to eat is more important than anything. I sometimes wonder whether, without Thi Ba, Mummy would let the old bep feed me at all. Everything I eat means that much less for her and Natalie.

The old bep is fond of me, I think, but like everyone else he's frightened of Mummy. And he doesn't love me enough to give me his own rations. He's hungry. Nobody loves anybody enough to eat less when they're as hungry as this.

Once I was so hungry I went and stole a little out of the tin of Nestlé's milk in the fridge, only I got caught and Mummy beat me so hard that it hurt for several days. Apparently I'm a horrible beast, I'm selfish and I don't think about other people who are even hungrier than me because they're bigger. Obviously if she'd killed me when she had the chance, instead of listening to the white wizard, she'd have more to eat now. I'm sure she was thinking of that when she was beating me. All the time she was hitting me, though, I tried not to cry, or at least not too loudly. I kept telling myself I was alive, at any rate, and that made me feel pleased.

When you're alive there are lots of things you can do. Go out into the street, for one. The street is marvellous: there are people everywhere. All the women look like Thi Ba. They wear the same black silk trousers under a long dress with a slit at the side, and they have the same shiny ball of black hair on the back of their neck. The men are as tall as Mummy, and no fatter. There are lots of children who run about all over the place without anyone stopping them. They have bare feet and torn and dirty clothes and they spit on the ground. I'm not allowed to do that. It's forbidden. Everything that's fun is forbidden.

When I was little, Thi Ba and I did lots of things that are forbidden. She took me to the market and bought me sweets full of germs. Germs are little animals that you can't see. When you eat too many of them you die, but they're delicious, much better than the bep's cooking. Sometimes Thi Ba used to stop at a soup-seller's stall. The cai bat was hot and burned my fingers and inside was thick white liquid with bits of food in it. I'd blow on it and it would all move around. If I blew too hard the soup overflowed and ran away. If I was good, Thi Ba also used to give me cold sweet potatoes. You were supposed to take the skin off with your nails, but my nails weren't long enough so Thi Ba used to help me. It was better when she did it, because when I tried to do it myself I got a lot of potato skin in my mouth and it was hard to swallow. But anyway they were good. Thi Ba didn't have much money, and I had none at all, so before we went out we used to search the house to see if there were any stray piastres. Thi Ba says that if people leave their money lying about it's because they don't really need it, so you can take it, it's not a bad thing. But people are so stupid they'd get angry anyway, so it's like everything else, you have to be careful they don't notice.

With the money we found we used to do lots of interesting things. But Thi Ba never takes me out now. The garden is closed off by soldiers and we aren't allowed out, although Mummy goes for a ride sometimes and Daddy still goes to work. Thi Ba says it's very dangerous because of the Viet Minh. This must be a Makoui who is even worse than the others, since he makes people cry as soon as he is mentioned. But apparently he's not a genie, so if the Viet Minh had to fight the Thân he would definitely lose.

I hate being shut up. I can play with the grey lizards who run all over the walls and ceiling but it's not so much fun as the street. Daddy and Mummy never want you to disturb them. Once Mummy got very angry. I'd gone into her room. I thought she was out and I wanted to steal some kumquats. There always used to be some in a white metal box hidden in her bedside table. There is so little to eat now I don't know if she still keeps kumquats in there. I went in without knocking. Mummy was standing in the middle of the room. She had lifted her dress up to her waist, as if she was going to do a pee. She was wearing a very funny pair of big pink knickers with laces at the front like on Daddy's shoes. Under the laces was a revolver. I asked who she wanted to kill. She pulled her dress down very quickly and shouted at me that I was talking nonsense. She said it wasn't a revolver, it was a kind of medicine for the tummy-ache she had. I know it was a revolver; they're easy to recognise because all the soldiers have them. When she'd finished shouting, Mummy explained to me that whites were forbidden to carry revolvers. You can go to prison and they cut your throat. So I swore not to say anything, not even to Thi Ba.

Sometimes, when Mummy is really horrible, I tell myself that if I was like her I could try to get her killed by someone else. It'd be easy. No need to get a yellow wizard, only the Makouis. I often wonder, though, how she has managed it so the Makouis don't notice that she goes about with a revolver against her stomach.

I could play with Natalie, but I'm only five and that isn't enough for her. She's twelve, so she's nearly a grown-up. And anyway she doesn't like dolls. She says that Sen, my little daughter, is very ugly. That's not true: Sen would be very pretty if she wasn't losing her hair. If I could I'd cut all Natalie's hair off, then she'd see what she looked like without it.

When Thi Ba gave me Sen, when I was very little, Sen was really beautiful. She had a blue Chinese dress with red flowers on it. The Makouis stole the dress. Thi Ba made another one out of an old nightie that was too small, and it's not so good. There are no red flowers any more.

The first time Natalie said Sen was hideous, I cried. And then I thought for a while. I went into Mummy's bathroom and stole some scissors and I cut my hair on both sides of my face. Not at the back, because that was too difficult. I tried to stick the hair on to Sen with some glue I stole from Daddy, but it didn't stay on. What's more my hair is fair and since Sen is Vietnamese it didn't suit her at all. I've tried to think where I can steal a dark doll to take its hair but I haven't found one. As time passes you find fewer things to steal. I'm scared of the day when the world is so poor there's nothing left to steal.

Thi Ba caught me; she was horrible and she went and told Mummy. I cried a lot and Thi Ba cut my hair at the back. Then she told me that my father had lost some of his hair too and nobody thought he was ugly because of it. She threw my hair away and she tied Sen's head up in a pretty pink handkerchief she'd gone and stolen somewhere else.

I'd like to find somebody to play with. Thi Ba hasn't got time. Natalie keeps on saying nasty things. She shuts herself in her room and when I want to come in she says, 'Go away; you can't even read!' When Thi Ba goes out without me Mummy orders me to go and play with Natalie, even if Natalie doesn't want me to. So I stay by myself.

When I get really bored, I take off my clothes and stand in front of the big mirror in my bedroom. My body is in two parts: all white where the clothes have been and all brown everywhere else. I don't know how I can get to be the colour of buddha. Neither of my two colours is right. Mummy says that I'm tanned and I'm hideous. Thi Ba says I'll never be a real yellow person, there's nothing to be done about it. Mummy and Natalie are as white on their outside bits as they are under their clothes. They always stay in the shade or go for walks under parasols. Mummy says it's only peasants and poor people who don't have the money to stay white. And idiots who want to copy them and lose their privileges. I don't know what privileges are, but I don't like the shade, or parasols. And anyway I haven't got any money and it's something that's difficult to steal.

When I'm fed up with thinking about how to be yellow, I get dressed again and I feel bored. Once I ran away. Everyone was having their afternoon sleep; Thi Ba was in the servants' house. I crept downstairs in my bare feet and saw that all the soldiers in the garden were asleep with their caps over their faces. I went out as quickly as I could and I ran.

It wasn't as much fun as it is with Thi Ba. There was hardly anyone in the street. The rickshaws had all stopped, and the coolies were asleep underneath them to get some shade. The sun was very heavy. My skin hurt, and my feet burned and stuck to the pavement. I looked at the cars but they weren't very pretty, and anyway I don't like cars. As soon as you get into one you feel ill. The only pretty cars are the ones with dead people inside, all black with decorations and flowers. In the end I'd had enough and I did the same as everyone else: I sat down against a wall and went to sleep.

It was an old gentleman with huge wrinkles on his thin legs who woke me up. He asked me, in French, if my parents were dead. I said, 'Not yet.' He wanted to know

18

where I lived and I said, 'In the big white house with the garden closed off by soldiers.' He laughed; apparently there are lots of houses like that. He also wanted to know my name and then Mummy and Daddy's names. But Henry and Charlotte weren't enough for him, he wanted another name and he didn't understand what I told him.

He said the streets were very dangerous. The yellow people wanted to kill all the French people and I mustn't stay there. I asked him if he wanted to kill me, too, but he was Chinese and he liked the French. So he took me with him.

He held my hand and we walked much too far. I was very thirsty and I wanted to call the water-seller but I didn't know whether the gentleman had any piastres.

I would have liked just to stay and sleep in the place where he'd found me, but I couldn't because he would have been unhappy about that. I went on walking. My whole body felt tired. The old gentleman kept on and on saying, 'We're nearly there,' but it was never true.

Finally, in a street which he told me had only Chinese people in it, we went into a little low house that didn't even have a top storey. There was only one room inside, and no floor, just earth like in my garden. Squatting children played with pieces of wood. The lady looked like Thi Ba, but she had bare feet and her hair was loose. She didn't have a dress over her black trousers. She pointed her finger at me and began to shout some words very fast. The gentleman listened to her calmly, and from time to time spoke a few words in a yellow language that was not the same as Thi Ba's. I wanted to leave and go home, but the old gentleman had told me to stay and play with the other children. I tried to do as he said but they turned their backs on me, so I picked up a rag doll whose arm someone had torn off and

19

then they all started shouting at me. They took the doll away and began to hit me. The old gentleman got angry then. He began to shout as well, and the children all ran away.

The noise woke the two bâ-gias curled up asleep on a mat deep inside the house. They immediately started shouting too. The old gentleman lifted his arms in the air and told me we'd have to leave. I was quite happy; I'd had enough of that house.

In the street, the old gentleman kissed me. He said I was a very pretty little girl. I had such soft skin and such fair hair and I smelled so good. He was very sorry that he couldn't keep me. As for me, I really liked the old gentleman, he was terribly kind, but I wouldn't have liked to live in his house. The lady didn't want anything to do with me and the children would have hit me. I explained all this to him and he said I was right.

We kept walking until we found a big white house with a garden closed off by soldiers. It looked like my house, but it wasn't. The old gentleman talked to the soldiers and we went inside. In the house was a very fat French lady all dressed in white, even her shoes. The old gentleman told her he'd found me in the street. The lady was horrible. She said we were disturbing her, and she wanted the old gentleman to put me in a home for abandoned children.

I wasn't at all happy about that. I said I had a Mummy, a Daddy, and even a Natalie, and a house like hers only bigger and prettier, with a swimming pool, lots of servants and two cars. I told her what my name was, and what Mummy and Daddy were called. The lady suddenly became very sweet. She told the old gentleman she knew who my parents were: they were very important people.

She made me sit down. She called her Thi Nam and asked

20

her to bring me a glass of cold water and a moon cake. I don't know how this lady still managed to have cake, but it was very good. When she went off to telephone I ate it all.

The lady came back smiling all over her face, like an image of buddha. She said my parents were going to come and get me and that the old gentleman should wait: he would get a reward.

The old gentleman squatted down next to my armchair but the lady got angry: 'No, no, not in my living room,' and sent him outside. I wanted to follow him but the lady wouldn't let me. I had to stay with her. It isn't much fun having to obey ladies just because they are grown-ups. When I'm grown up I'll let little girls do anything they want. Unless they are Natalies.

The lady talked a lot, and asked lots of questions. She wanted to know why I didn't go to school. She wanted me to go to her school. She would teach me to read and write. I asked whether Natalie would play with me if I went to school but she didn't know. She also talked about the church and I asked if that was a mountain, like the Tam Dao. The lady let out a shriek. She said it was an absolute disgrace and I'd said a terrible thing.

I was furious. I decided to leave and go and find the old gentleman again. I slid out of the armchair, but the lady caught me by the arm and sat me down very roughly. I sulked and didn't say anything else. Luckily then Mummy and Daddy arrived in the black car with Kao, the chauffeur. Mummy was in a dreadful state. She wanted to know what I was doing there. I explained I'd wanted to go for a walk and then I couldn't find the house again. Daddy said horrible things about Thi Ba. She was incapable of looking after me and he was going to give her the sack. I started to cry. I said that if Thi Ba left I would go with her. Mummy made a great speech. She said, 'If Thi Ba gets the sack, it'll be your fault. We won't fire her this time, but the next time you go out of the house alone I promise you Thi Ba will have to leave straight away.'

I stopped crying and the fat lady sent for the old gentleman. Daddy gave him some piastres and he was all happy. He went out of the room backwards, bowing in little dips to the front as he went.

I wanted to go too, and to get home to Thi Ba again, but I can never do what I want. Daddy and Mummy sat down with the French lady and Thi Nam served them with tea and some chocolate buns, because this lady seemed to have all sorts of cakes. I fell asleep in the yellow armchair and dreamed about the dragon again. I was running up the white staircase in the house and he was chasing me, spitting flames from his mouth. I was afraid. I ran and ran, but the staircase never came to an end and the dragon was always behind me, huge and blue. I was only as big as one of his teeth.

Mummy woke me up before the staircase ended and I had to say thank you to the lady. Then we left.

In the car Mummy didn't speak to me but when we arrived at the house she slapped me very hard. She said I was lucky not to be dead and the next time she wouldn't come to get me. She had had enough of my stupid behaviour. She went on about the day I almost drowned. If Natalie hadn't laughed at me because she knows how to swim and I don't I wouldn't have jumped into the pool, and Kao wouldn't have torn his clothes when he came to get me out of the water which meant that Daddy had to give him some money to buy new ones. So. It's always my fault.

When Mummy finally stopped yelling, Thi Ba kissed me and kissed me. She even got permission to sleep in my room for the night. We both pretended I was feeling ill and the number one boy put up a folding bed for her beside mine. But the next day I looked as if I was in perfect health and she had to go back and sleep with the other servants.

I love it when Thi Ba comes to sleep with me. To begin with, I don't feel frightened, and also she explains a lot of things to me. The fat lady's church, for example, is apparently a rather ugly sort of pagoda, with a thin white false buddha that French people go and pray to. They give him piastres to buy their way to Nirvana. I don't understand why since the white people started off by torturing him and killing him because he was a false buddha. And now they go and pray to him and give him money. Thi Ba says it's pointless to try and understand, white people are all mad anyhow.

I'm hungry. There's nothing to steal in the kitchen, though. There hasn't been anything for a long time. This year the bep didn't make anything for Tet. It was no fun at all; the New Year was just a day like any other.

When I was little we had all sorts of delicious things to eat. Nems, for example. The bep used to cut them up with scissors, and we mixed them with mint leaves and lettuce before dipping them in nuoc-mâm. I often wake up at night and think about the taste it made when the nem cracked between my teeth and all the soft bit inside filled my mouth. We also had ban cuon abssi, all white like the skin of white people kept well in the shade, and all soft. Ban cuons are the hardest things in the world to eat. They're too big to put in your mouth all at once but they break between the pieces of bread and all the stuffing goes everywhere. What I liked too were big fat cakes of gluey rice stuffed with pork

23

and wrapped in banana leaves. They cooked for hours in the boiling pan. I used to climb on a stool and watch the water moving about. The bep would pretend to shout at me and tell me I wasn't supposed to be in the kitchen, but there wasn't anywhere I was supposed to be, nobody ever wanted me, and besides I knew the bep was only teasing. The proof was that he never hit me. But all this was a long time ago. Even the soya milk that fed me when I was a baby, because there wasn't any real milk and Mummy didn't have any, or wanted to keep it all for herself, I don't know which, even soya milk doesn't exist any more. If I'd known that being able to eat as much as you wanted would stop so soon, I'd have eaten much more.

My daughter Sen is too little; she never knew the time when you could really eat. Because of that, she misses it less since she doesn't know what it's like.

'Tiet zoi! I left Sen outside, in the hut beside the pool!'

I shouldn't have spoken out loud. It's dangerous. You must always be on the lookout. If Mummy knew that I could speak several words of Annamese, swear-words what's more, she'd be furious. She doesn't want me to learn any. She thinks the Indochinese always say terrible things and Thi Ba has been ordered only to speak to me in French.

How can I have forgotten Sen? It's the first time I've done it. She must be very sad. She certainly thinks I'm a bad mother. I have no right to behave badly to Sen because I wanted her. She isn't an unwanted child.

Sen must be frightened, all alone in the dark. But there's no danger. Not at the moment. The Japanese soldiers have stayed in the street, and we haven't heard the bomb sirens that sometimes scream so loudly in the middle of the night. When they howl out you have to run very very fast, in just the knickers you sleep in, and you're allowed to go barefoot.

Then you go into the cellar, under the ground, and you wait in the dark.

I'm wrong, there's always a danger: the Makouis. The Makouis hide in the dark so they can do more mischief.

Luckily, now I'm not four any more, I'm nearly grown up. I don't need anyone.

I didn't put the light on, because you have to do that kind of thing in secret. How do blind people manage to walk? It's very hard. I almost missed the first step of the staircase. The next ones were easier because I held on to the banister. I opened my eyes very wide but it didn't help.

I've found out how to do it. It's better to pretend to be really blind and put your hands out in front of you.

The front door is so heavy; I have to push it with my whole body.

What bad luck: the moon was playing hide and seek.

'Tiet zoi!' The Makoui pushed me and I fell over. There was a sudden cold draught and I slid onto one of the flowerpots. I hurt myself. I'm scared. I shouldn't have sworn; the Thâns won't protect me now. If I get up, the Makoui will see I'm alive and he'll kill me.

I'll play a trick on him: I'll pretend to be dead and crawl as far as the hut.

It hurts more now. The flowerpot broke and cut both my knees, and since I have to crawl the gravel is getting into the cuts.

It's hard to look as if you're dead and keep moving forward all the same. I go very slowly. It hurts too much; it's difficult not to cry. If only Thi Ba was here. No, it's better that she's not, or the Makoui might hurt her.

Please, Thân genies, look after Sen. How could I have forgotten her? If the Makoui has taken her away, I'll just stand up and let him kill me.

25

This is such a long path. It's like the dragon staircase; it has no end.

So as not to cry you have to try to think about nothing. I'm there now. Where is the bench? Where's Sen? I can't see anything. I'll have to stand up, but it's dangerous because the Makoui will see I'm still alive. I can't bend my knees any longer. There's the bench; I've just touched it. I grab hold of it and try to pull myself up. Sen doesn't want to come with me. She slides out of my hand.

That's it; I've got her. Now I've got to run, get back to the house, shut us both in. I'm standing up but everything around me is moving. The dragon must be stirring. I'm dizzy. I feel sick, worse than in a car, but I mustn't vomit.

I'm running, limping. Sen is squeezed tight against me; she's frightened. The Makoui is chasing us, blowing burning air all over us.

I try to push the door open, but the Makoui is pushing it very hard the other way. It's so difficult . . . I shout, 'Thi Ba! Thi Ba!' . . . and push again. Sen wants to cry, terribly badly. I can't stand up any more. The Makoui is stopping my breath. I'm slipping. I mustn't – the Makoui will take Sen – I'm slipping. How long does it take to die? I'm slipping and slipping. I can't breathe at all. Thi Ba isn't coming.

There is one great blow, and I fall down dead.

Mummy is standing beside my bed. With her hair all loose she looks like someone else's mother. As she talks to the doctor she gives great sighs, like the bep when he's not happy.

Mummy woke me up and carried me to my bed. She wanted to take Sen away from me but I screamed and she let me keep hold of her. Mummy was very funny. She was crying like other people do.

I want Thi Ba. Daddy has gone to the servants' house to get her.

The doctor is wrapping my knees in long bands of cloth cut from some net curtains. He's telling Mummy about a dragon called Hiroshima which has thrown flames over the Japanese and destroyed everything.

'That's impossible,' Mummy says, and she's in the state she gets into when the bombing starts.

Apparently we aren't going to go to the concentration camps now. The Japanese were so frightened of the dragon that they've all run away.

Mummy says that without Hiroshima we would all have been killed.

Should I pray to Hiroshima? I must ask Thi Ba.

Daddy comes back alone. He says to Mummy: 'Thi Ba has run away. She went with Kao and the car. She's taken all her things.'

They're lying. Or else they're joking, just pretending. Thi Ba hasn't gone without taking me. I can't stop crying. I hurt all over, I want Thi Ba.

'I'm here,' Mummy says, 'don't cry.'

But I don't care whether Mummy is there or not.

'She was afraid,' the doctor says.

'That's no reason to steal the car.' Mummy is getting angry.

Has Thi Ba gone to Africa without me?

'Stop that crying,' Mummy says. 'There's no point. If she loved you she would have stayed. She didn't love you.'

She didn't love me.

CHAPTER TWO

Since the dragon made Thi Ba and the Japanese run away, Mummy has decided to take my education in hand. Having my education taken in hand makes me cry a lot; I hate being slapped. But I have lots of freedom. The only problem is to guess what time meals are. Mealtimes are very important because that's when the education happens. Natalie and I aren't allowed to eat with my parents; we're too little, even Natalie. You have to wait until you're fifteen. In the evenings we have dinner in the little dining room, and the number one boy serves us. Mummy stands up so that she can watch us better. The most difficult part is using the knife and fork. Thi Ba never showed me how and I'm not allowed chopsticks any more. Mummy shouts the whole time that I'm not doing what I'm supposed to do, but since we have less and less to eat it doesn't last very long. What's also difficult is not to tread on my dress. Natalie and I each have a long dress specially made by the number two seamstress (she's less expensive, but what she makes isn't good enough for Mummy to wear). Every evening we have to put them on until we go to bed. It's so that we get used to it. When we're eighteen, we're going to come out into society and we'll have to dress like that. Apparently if you're not used to it, you don't have the right gestures and you look ridiculous. Natalie never steps on her dress, since it only comes down as far as the top of her feet, but mine drags along the ground and I have a lot of trouble with all the extra material. Mummy says it's a dress that'll last me while I'm growing. But I'd be amazed if it lasted me until I'm eighteen.

I'd like to know what coming out into society is. When I ask Mummy she tells me not to ask such silly questions. Before, Thi Ba used to explain everything to me, but since Mummy is a white person she doesn't have to take any notice of children. Anyway, she's not paid to. I'm not really a proper white person because I often go barefoot and I haven't got the right gestures. But I'm not a yellow person. It's a terrible bother; I don't know what I am.

As soon as I get the chance I dash out into the street. I sit on the ground, in a place I like, beside other people. I pretend to be mute so that they won't notice I don't speak like they do. I stay there for a long time watching them and I feel very happy. I rub my bare feet in the dust and I think of lots of things.

I'm waiting for the war to be over so Thi Ba can come back. It might be a very long time, a year at least, but I don't mind, I'll wait.

In a year I'll be seven. I was six a few days ago. I had a real birthday, just as if Thi Ba was here. There were six white candles on top of a moon cake. Six candles is a lot; there was hardly any room left on the cake. Natalie had the largest bit. Mummy says she is bigger than me and should eat more. But it wasn't her birthday! I think that on your birthday you should be allowed to eat more than other people. The old bep has promised me that soon we'll be able to have cake whenever we want. If they're big cakes I won't mind if Natalie gets more than me.

The great bore is that some white people have moved in with us. The guest house is full of people who've lost their own houses. And all these white people want to eat.

Mummy has no more jewellery to exchange for food. There are only piastres left, and piastres aren't worth enough to buy food.

In the guest house there's a fat lady who is always trying to slip into the kitchen to see if she can make the bep give her a bit extra, but Mummy keeps an eye on her and she never gets there. There's also a very grand gentleman who smiles all the time and who Natalie follows everywhere. And then there is the wife of the gentleman who gets furious when she sees Natalie talking to her husband.

The saddest one is the lady who cries all the time, even at table when you give her something to eat. Whenever she sees me she cries even louder, and Mummy has forbidden me to go near her. Apparently she had a Laurence the same age as me who was killed at the same time as the house. The lady scares me; I'm sure she's mad. Everyone knows you don't cry about a Laurence.

Thi Ba used to say you have to watch out for mad people. They don't like life, and that's very dangerous for them and for other people too.

With all these extra unwanted people, I play at being dumb and invisible.

Mummy has explained to them that I am a wild animal. Apparently when I was very little, if a white person wanted to take me in their arms I used to bite them. Mummy would hit me, but Thi Ba used to stick up for me. She'd say I was frightened, and that was why. It's quite normal to be frightened. I can't remember if the feeling was stronger than usual, but I hate it when people I don't like take hold of me as if I was a thing that belonged to them. No one should be allowed to do that – except to dead people who can't be troubled by it any more. If wild animals defend themselves, they've got good reason. If I'd been bigger at the time, I'd have thought up ways to protect myself. For example, I could have said I had a contagious disease and then nobody would have dared touch me. But I was too little to know what you have to do. Thi Ba hadn't taught me to lie to protect myself then. Thi Ba explained everything so well. When I told lies badly she corrected me and showed me how I could have done it much better. She said that when you can lie perfectly, you always get away with things. Now there's no one to teach me how to live properly.

It's really tiring waiting for Thi Ba to come back.

Mummy keeps saying she's going to find a way for us to leave and go to France. She has objects and pieces of furniture wrapped up ready to send over. But I don't want to go. They can go without me. Otherwise Thi Ba will never be able to find me again. I don't say anything though. It's not worth getting yourself scolded before you have to. I'll just run away at the last moment. The town is so big, there are lots of places I could hide. They'll think I'm dead.

I must start looking for a good hiding place.

When I feel really sad and can't wait for it to stop, because it's useless sadness, I go to the pagoda. It's very beautiful and you can stay there as long as you want without paying. What I like best is the buddha who is so golden he looks as if he's made of sunshine, and so big that nobody can look him in the face. And his smile – as if he really loves us and doesn't even have to lie.

When I first get there I feel so bad I can't even see how beautiful it is, but little by little I start to breathe more easily. That pagoda is such a peaceful place that apart from the people crying you could forget that life can be so sad.

I wonder whether pagodas can be killed like ordinary houses. I think they probably can, otherwise everyone would go and live in them. But there wouldn't be enough room, unless they put pagodas everywhere. The only thing is that in a pagoda you must never do anything that's not allowed, and you can't get through your whole life without ever doing anything that's forbidden. So after a while all the people would go off to do stupid things somewhere else, and they'd get themselves killed. That must be why there are so few pagodas. You just go there from time to time to make yourself feel better, then you go away again to play or to look for something to eat.

In the end, pagodas are less important than they seem. There are only three really important things: being alive, having something to eat and finding someone who loves you.

When Thi Ba comes back I'll ask her to take me to the seaside. To Do Sohn, where we've already been, so long ago that I can't remember when it was. But this time we won't take Mummy or Natalie with us; Daddy isn't a problem because he never came anyway.

When we were at Do Sohn, it was as beautiful as the pagoda and even more wonderful because we could do all the things we aren't allowed to do, as long a̩ ̩e didn't get caught, of course.

At Do Sohn we stayed in a house on stilts and we felt like birds in a tree. I could look down on everything from high up, as if I was the buddha, and I felt I could see much further than I can from the ground. The top of the house was a safe place. The proof was that when the sea was pushed up by the monsoon and decided to invade the earth (which doesn't belong to her) and make war on it, the water all rose up with a loud shriek, but it couldn't reach the top of the house. It was so beautiful that I came down as far as the sitting-room terrace and I had sea water all around my legs. It was Thi Ba who came to get me and she shouted even louder than the water, because I should have stayed in my room and not moved. But my room didn't have a terrace and I couldn't see so well. I had to go back up just the same; apparently I might have died and the sea can kill you as easily as bombs can.

I really wonder if there is anything you couldn't get yourself killed with if you didn't watch out.

On the whole white people don't know how to watch out for things. Daddy, for example. One day I saw him fighting with a knife. It was astonishing because Daddy isn't like Mummy, he never seems to get angry. I don't know why he was so furious that day, white people always refuse to explain things to children, but I managed to watch because nobody noticed me. Daddy was much taller and broader than the yellow man, but he was so clumsy that in the end it was him who got wounded.

Whites are stupid, they trust people. In Hanoi there are whole families of white people who die because they trust their bep and eat whatever they're given without thinking. So the bep takes advantage of that to poison them with datura. Usually the beps are paid to do it, and they all need money. But the whites don't take precautions. They don't make the bep eat a bit of what he has cooked before they eat it, and watch him while he does it. At home, the bep always tastes things in front of us. He's quite happy to do it, too: it means he gets a little more food.

The trouble is it means less for us.

White people have another fault: they get mixed up in things which aren't their business. That's also dangerous.

One day, I was peacefully asleep on my bit of pavement, not asking anything of anybody. I love that piece of pavement; I know the people who come and sit there. They always make a little space for me. We don't speak to each other, we just smile. When I have a few piastres more than I need just for myself I buy them a little water. When they have a bit more water than they need they give me some. We're well organised.

That day I was happy enough, except I hadn't been able to find any piastres to steal and the people around me didn't have anything either, so we were all rather thirsty. The water-seller kept coming past, to make us want it more, but we pretended we weren't thirsty anyway. He was crafty, though, that water-seller, and he knew very well we had no money.

Then a white lady came by, a lady I'd seen at home. When she saw me she stopped and stared at me from under her big white hat, very crossly, and said: 'What are you doing here? Go home at once! It's very dangerous to hang about the streets like this.'

I didn't answer, of course. I pretended she didn't exist. She got very angry. I was so frightened when I saw her behaving just like Mummy I started to cry, so the yellow people around me got up, one by one, in silence, and began to make a circle around her. When she saw what was happening, she got scared and ran away. The yellow people stood aside to let her go and then went and sat down again.

At least that lady had learned to look out for herself. If she hadn't run away she'd be dead. I've already seen that happen. If a white person is alone on the street and gets angry with a yellow person, all the other yellow people nearby surround the white person. When there are enough of them they pick up stones from the ground and throw them at the white person.

There was a time when the whites didn't have to watch out for themselves: the yellow people were too scared of them. When a white man got out of a rickshaw he paid whatever he wanted. Even if it wasn't enough. Now the whites pay what the coolie asks for, they daren't argue.

34

The whites who die from the stones are the ones who shout at yellow people just like they used to, because they don't understand that it's dangerous now.

As for me, what I liked about the business with the lady was that the people on my bit of pavement behaved as if I was yellow. I'd become a friend.

Ever since the Japanese, who are yellow people from the same race as the Makouis, went away, I feel safe in the street. Mummy says I've got a hide like a rhinoceros because I'm not afraid. But white people don't know that when you're afraid you must never show it, it's not an honourable emotion. You must always hide what is not fine. It seems to me that whites lie much less than yellow people, but you must always lie when you want to behave in an honourable way. Otherwise it means that the person you're talking to isn't important. White people don't care. They show themselves as they are and then they're astonished that people don't like them.

When I see how Natalie behaves, at her age, I feel ashamed for her. Before the Hiroshima dragon, bombs used to fall at night and each time the warning siren sounded she'd start to scream and cry and run off to hide in a cupboard or under a bed.

At those times I used to tell myself I didn't care that Natalie wouldn't play with me. It's all very well that she knows how to read and I don't, but she wouldn't even have been able to die in an honourable way. That's what Thi Ba said and Thi Ba is always right.

While I'm waiting to die an honourable death, as late as I can, I get very hungry. It's really annoying to be hungry all the time. You can't think of anything else. Even inside the pagoda, the hunger is still there. I'd love a bit of chocolate. Chocolate is Nirvana. I had some when the white soldiers came. I used to think that only yellow people could be soldiers, but no, these were proper soldiers and they were white. They paraded in big jeeps and tanks, with their heads sticking a long way out of the top. They were huge, with very white faces and caps and smiles. The whole town crowded onto the pavements, clapping wildly. People waved their hands and handkerchiefs and flags. People shouted. It was as beautiful as a pagoda. The only sad thing was that Thi Ba wasn't there to see it.

The soldiers were happy. They threw all sorts of strange things at us. It was wonderful: they were all things you could eat! There was chocolate in little pieces and big chunks, each wrapped up in two bits of paper, one with colours and patterns on it and the other one silver. Everyone was fighting to get some. Sometimes I won. You had to eat it fast, before somebody grabbed it from you. It was soft. I didn't know what it was, I only found out afterwards what it was called, so I just copied other people. You had to tear off the coloured paper and lick the other one. Then so as not to miss any of it you licked your hands as well, and you swallowed bits of silver paper and earth at the same time. Everyone fell over, of course, while they were fighting, and my arms and legs got covered with bruises and blood. But it wasn't the kind of blood that makes you die, or means you have to go to hospital.

They also threw us chewing-gum. At first I didn't know it was like betel: you're supposed to chew it then spit it out. I swallowed it. It wasn't very good, but I ate it anyway.

They threw metal cans, too, with milk in them, or food all ready-made. These were good but very complicated. I couldn't open them myself, so I had to take them back to the house and get Mummy to cut them open with a special knife. This took up a lot of time and made me lose my place in the front row. I had to fight to get back there again.

While I was gone they went on throwing things. I was furious at having to go away. It wasn't fair. Mummy and Natalie ate some of everything but they wouldn't come and help me. They just stayed put and waited. I even gave them some of the chocolate, although I didn't have to: I could open that on my own. They knew what chocolate was, that's how I found out its name.

Mummy counted the cans. I'd done really well; there were more than ten. We only ate two straight away. Mummy locked the rest up in a cupboard. I could have got more, but suddenly one of the soldiers got down onto the pavement. He lifted me in his arms, climbed back up on top of his tank and sat me down beside him.

It was marvellous. Much more beautiful than a funeral. He gave me some chocolate all to myself. New chocolate, not squashed at all. He told me lots of things, but there was so much noise I could hardly hear. He spoke French with a foreign accent and I couldn't understand it all. He stroked my hair as gently as Thi Ba used to before she went away. The tank moved forward slowly. I wanted it to keep going for ever. I was happy. I was on parade. I was with the people everyone was clapping for, the people who had things to eat.

That soldier was wonderful. He looked like all the others, very tall, very white, with a uniform and a cap, but he was much more handsome. And he had green eyes, so green they glittered like shooting stars made of jade. So I wished very hard, all alone in my head, that Thi Ba would come back, because I was sure eyes like that must be able to bring happiness. I had never seen such beautiful eyes. Yellow people never have green eyes, and white people usually have black or brown or blue eyes. Thi Ba used to say I had some green in my eyes, but it's mixed with other colours and that's not the same.

I felt so proud. That soldier, who was as honourable as a buddha, had chosen me; he had put me beside him. I tried to make him like me. I combed my hair with my fingers and I rubbed at my knees. We talked. Or rather I talked a great deal. He asked lots of questions, and I answered when I could understand him. It was difficult for me not to put Annamese words in my language, it was very annoying. I'd never spoken to a white person for so long. I tried to tell him about Hanoi, about Thi Ba, Mummy and even Natalie. At one moment he hugged me against him and kissed me very hard on my left cheek, just on the bone. At night before I go to sleep I touch the place where I felt his mouth. Sometimes it makes me want to cry. For several days I managed not to wash there without anyone noticing, but one morning the bep said my face was dirty and gave it a soaping, and I didn't dare say anything.

After a while the soldier took a notebook out of his pocket, tore out a page and wrote all over one side, then all over the other. He asked me to take it to Mummy as quickly as possible. He lifted me up and put me on the ground. He smiled, and gave a last stroke to my hair, and said, 'I'll be waiting for you,' but without saying where, or when. Then he went away on top of his tank, which was still moving slowly along the street. He turned back once, waving his arm, then he disappeared with the others.

I looked hard at the piece of paper from all sides, but I don't know how to read. Thi Ba taught me to count up to ten, but that was no use. So I ran all the way home, holding the piece of paper squeezed tightly between my fingers.

Mummy wouldn't read it. She didn't have time. I went to see Daddy. I had to wait for ages, but in the end he told me what was on it. There was the name and address of the soldier, who was a captain, here in Hanoi but also in France, in a town called Strasbourg. He said he wanted to adopt me, he had plenty of money, and that I would be very happy with him over there in France. I didn't care about the money, because you can always manage to steal a bit, and I didn't like the idea of living in France, but I wanted so much never to leave him, my soldier, that I would have gone anywhere, even to Japan, with him. I asked: 'Does he want me? Really want me?'

It was unbelievable, but it was true. Daddy said yes, he did. I asked if I could go straight away. Daddy got angry then. I was a heartless monster, I'd leave them just like that for a complete stranger. Anyway, the soldier was making fun of me. He was joking.

He called Mummy and she got angry too. She tore up the piece of paper without even reading it.

I don't understand. Why didn't they give me to the soldier? Neither Daddy or Mummy have ever wanted me and anyway they'd have more to eat if I was gone. Why couldn't they give me to someone who wanted me? Mummy said, 'It's just not done.'

It's probably not allowed. Like stealing or telling lies. But if you don't make up your mind to do things that aren't allowed you'll never be happy.

Every day I go back to the place where the soldiers paraded. I tell myself that perhaps the Strasbourg soldier will want to see me again and he'll take it into his head to come and look for me at the place he found me before. I don't know if that could happen, but I try. I think as hard as I can. I'd like to belong to the soldier, but it's terribly difficult because I don't even know his name and I'm not clever enough to think of a way to find him.

If Thi Ba was here she'd know what to do. But since she went away everything is all jumbled up in my head. As I can't talk to anyone the ideas stay crowded in my mind like the ghosts on the back of the old tiger, and all those questions without answers make me feel very tired.

So I just wait there, hoping to see the soldier, but I'm not really sure which bit of the pavement he picked me up from. I move from time to time, more or less at random. I feel very upset because I think if he remembers just where it was he might be angry to see that I've made a mistake and haven't waited for him in exactly the right place.

There's another problem, too. I'm scared I won't recognise him. I only know that he's very tall, very white, with very green eyes, but since I've started looking at all white men in case they might be him I've realised there are other white men like that. This makes things much more complicated because it means that he'd have to recognise me.

It's extremely difficult to love someone you don't know. For example, if he decides to come back and take me with him, I wouldn't want to arrive at his house empty-handed. I'd like to give him a present. But what present? What would a soldier like mine want? I have no idea and nobody can help me. Apart from guns or food, which he already has, I can't see what it would be. I've managed to steal a few piastres which I've hidden away for him, but I don't know how to recognise piastres and I don't know whether the ones I've got are important ones or not. Perhaps I've stolen badly and they're not important enough to buy anything good. I've never been into a shop to buy something and I've no idea about the price or how you should behave in places like that. All I know how to buy is water or food in the street, when there is any.

I've often wanted to spend those piastres, but I keep the need deep inside me. It's a thing I could never do, even when I've stood and waited so long that I'm cooking and I feel as if I'm dying of thirst when I see the water-seller go by.

I wonder where the water-seller gets the water he sells. Perhaps he steals it from the great lake, or the little lake? Thi Ba said that only white people and very rich yellow people have taps in their houses, with water that runs by itself. By the way, it's because it runs by itself, except when you shut it off, that you call that kind of water running water.

Since the water-seller is a poor yellow man, he can't have a tap in his house. When you're poor, everything you need belongs to somebody else. Are you allowed to steal water from the lakes? Or would the water-seller go to prison if the whites caught him? Thi Ba used to say, 'He very clever,' because she thought he charged too much, but nobody is clever all the time.

Water is a very important thing. That's why the poor people save rainwater whenever they can. You need lots of water to live. You need it to drink, but also to make food with. Nobody needs to wash, but if there wasn't any water in the paddyfields everyone would die.

Long ago, so many years ago that nobody knows when, there was a great drought which lasted such a long time that children became grown men without ever having seen water falling from the sky. It was horrifying. The earth turned to pebbles and men and animals became dry bones.

Almost everyone died and those who were still alive no longer even prayed to buddha.

The toad, even though he needs a lot of water, had somehow managed to survive, but he was so unhappy he

41

decided to go to heaven to complain and demand that the rains should come back again. He left one evening, at the coolest time, on the long road that leads to heaven, a dead straight road. On the way the toad met an old crab, who despite his great age didn't even know that rain existed. The toad explained to the crab what rain was and persuaded him to come along.

A little further on, the toad and the crab met a bee who was almost dying, so they put him on the back of the old man crab and took him with them.

They covered kilometres that seemed as long as life itself beneath a sun that burned like a red brick oven. The toad could no longer drag along his dried-up body. He moaned, 'The earth is losing her trees like an old man losing his hair. She's about to die.'

He was heard by a young tiger who had managed to stay alive. He came up to them, his tongue hanging out, and asked: 'Where are you going?'

'To heaven,' replied the yellow toad (he had been green before but the lack of water and the overflowing sun had changed his colour), 'to demand the return of the rain.'

'It's a long way,' the tiger sighed, 'and it's terribly hard to walk so far when you're thirsty, but I'll come with you.'

It is true that it's horribly difficult to climb the pebbly path that leads to heaven, but the toad was brave and knew how to set a good example. At long last all four of them arrived in front of the great gate of heaven, all golden like the gates of a pagoda. There the toad struck three bold strokes on the drum that serves as a doorbell. The Emperor of Heaven came out to see who it was that dared disturb him. He began to get angry, but the toad pleaded with him very cleverly.

'For years and years,' he said, 'the rain has stayed in the

air instead of falling to earth. We're all dying. Who will you have to reign over when we're all dead?'

'That's a point,' said the Emperor of Heaven, scratching his long white beard. 'I've been busy playing chess and I've forgotten all about the earth. I was wrong. From now on, whenever you need water, all the toad has to do is warn me by starting to croak. Then I'll order the water dragon to spit the rain over the earth.'

That's why there is rain now – because of the courage of the toad, who you must always respect if you don't want heaven to punish you by taking away the rain. It's thanks to the toad that the water-seller can earn a living. Otherwise there wouldn't be any more water in the world. Not even with taps. Later on, I'd like to be a water-seller. I think it's a fine profession, and you earn masses of piastres. There are so few people with taps that everyone needs the water-seller.

Also, I'd very much like to meet a toad some day. I've never seen one. Thi Ba said it was a bit like a lizard, but it doesn't run across the walls.

Mummy doesn't like the water-seller. She doesn't need him. At home, because we're a rich house, there are taps and you can drink all you want without paying. The problem is that I'm in the house very little and in the street a lot, and there I can't have a drink without piastres. It's stupid to pay for something when you're out if you can get it for nothing at home, but that's how it is. And besides I must say the water-seller's water is much nicer than the water in the taps.

I'm out much more since Thi Ba went away. Before, Thi Ba used to make me sleep in my room in the afternoons, but now I can have my afternoon rest in the street because no one cares where I am except at mealtimes. I prefer the

43

street. Even if I don't talk any more than I do at home, I'm never alone.

I've started thinking about chocolate again. Apparently I had some once before, when I was little. The sad thing is, however hard I try, I can't remember it, so it doesn't do me any good. I was nine or ten months old, Mummy can't remember exactly, and someone had given Natalie a chocolate chicken for Easter (I didn't dare ask her what Easter was). She was stupid enough to let me lick a little bit and of course I adored it. So when they left me alone, with the chicken still on the table, I wriggled about in my cot on wheels until I managed to move it up to the table. Once I got there, I grabbed the chicken and sucked it. When they came back, I had chocolate all over me and all over the cot sheets too. Mummy said she yelled a lot, which doesn't surprise me, and that I was a filthy beast even then.

Filthy beast: those were the first two words I learned to say. Mummy often reproaches me for it, but I didn't make them up. If she hadn't said them to me so often perhaps I wouldn't have learned to repeat them.

Thi Ba never called me a filthy beast. Thi Ba was always gentle, even when she was cross. I was really lucky that she agreed to stay with me so long, but it's sad my luck ran out so suddenly. You get used to feeling happy and then you can't do without it. Thi Ba used to say that white people can be happy more easily than yellow people, because yellow people are born to be poor. Being rich means you can have lots of taps and a big house with a bedroom for each person and objects everywhere. I couldn't care less about being rich, and anyway I loathe being alone in my bedroom. I prefer to be in the street with people all round me. But now I come to think about it, money's also useful for buying food, and the more money you have the more you can eat.

My soldier wrote on his piece of paper that he had plenty of money. I suppose in his country he has a big house with taps and an enormous amount of food too. I'm very happy for him. It's wonderful when you see nice things happening to someone you love. Usually it's the people you don't like who are allowed them.

I expect he eats chocolate every day, and maybe he even has enough to give some to other people. If he takes me with him one day, I'm sure he'll give me some. But I'll only take a tiny bit, so he can have more than me. I'd be very unhappy if he had to eat less because of me, especially since he must be used to eating a lot. Would he be in danger of having less food if he took me? That would be sad.

But when he said he had plenty of money, it was probably a way of explaining that he had enough piastres for us both to eat, and not just him alone.

Anyway, it doesn't matter. If he hasn't got enough piastres, I'll find a way not to cost him anything. I'll steal all my food; perhaps there's more food to steal in Strasbourg than there is in Hanoi. Everyone, or almost everyone, is hungry in Hanoi, so of course food is harder to steal than anything else.

I hope Thi Ba isn't hungry, wherever she is; I hope she's found someone to give her food. Perhaps she stayed with Kao, the chauffeur. He's a nice man, Kao. He never shouted at me and he used to speak kindly to me from time to time. I remember once I was hiding in a corner of the garden, crying, and he happened to find me; he took out his handkerchief to wipe my eyes. He said: 'It's all right. Nothing matters, you know.'

I was so embarrassed because he'd seen me crying that I

45

didn't even thank him for the handkerchief or the words. That was bad. People so rarely bother about you or talk to you, you mustn't forget to thank them.

Thi Ba used to bother about me, and talk to me. I wasn't very nice to her – I didn't thank her. Maybe that's why she went away. Since she went I haven't learned anything. It's very annoying, because now I don't know what's going on. I'd like someone to tell me whether the Japanese might come back and if the Viet Minh is still so dangerous. And whether the bombs are going to fall again. Also, I'd love some news of the Hiroshima dragon. I'm very fond of that dragon, because he saved our lives: without him I'd be dead and I'd never have met my soldier.

If I'm lucky enough to find my soldier again one day, I'll ask him to take me to make an offering to the Hiroshima dragon, to say thank you.

I wish I knew: do dragons like chocolate? It'd be a fine offering, if I knew where I could steal some. But I don't even know where I could offer it up to the Hiroshima dragon. Life is very difficult without Thi Ba.

One problem is going round in my mind: if I found a very tiny bit of chocolate, so small it couldn't be divided, would I be brave enough to give it to him? I'm afraid I wouldn't, afraid I'd just throw myself at it and gobble it up. In that case, what's the good of all my love for the soldier and for Thi Ba, and my gratitude to the Hiroshima dragon? Thinking about that tiny bit of chocolate makes me miserable.

What's so complicated about life is that you have to have enough for yourself but also enough for the people you love, and that's a lot to ask.

I dabble my bare feet in the dust and I think hard. Splaying my feet out on the pavement always helps me think. Sometimes at home when I ask myself complicated questions which have no answer, I go outside so that my feet can help me. The problem is, however hard I think, I don't get anywhere. I wish my soldier was here so I could talk to him about everything; he could tell me what I should do. Even if it meant I could never eat chocolate again, if it was him who decided it wouldn't matter.

I still can't understand what is important and what isn't. If nobody helps me I'm lost. Here everyone apart from me knows what to do, but I don't know how to do anything, except steal stray piastres. I remember how before, when the yellow people saw someone hurt or killed by the bombs, they used to pounce on them and take whatever they had. But I didn't move. Partly because I had no right, since I'm not yellow, and partly because it seemed pointless. Everything they took from the dead people was unimportant: watches, jewellery, shoes. Apart from wallets with piastres inside, there was nothing useful. I've never seen any food on a dead person.

I've got two pairs of sandals I hardly ever use, but no one would give me any chocolate in exchange for them. I've no jewellery and no watch. Anyway, I don't know how to tell the time, since nobody's taught me. If one day I learn how, I'll do what everyone else does: steal a watch. Even so I wouldn't do much with it, because apart from mealtimes it would be no use.

I didn't think to notice whether my soldier had a watch, but I suppose he's rich enough to have one which wasn't even stolen. Thi Ba had one that was taken from a dead person, but it wasn't the right sort of dead person, she said, because the watch was too big and very ugly, a poor man's watch.

Mummy used to have several very expensive watches,

47

but they were turned into food which has already been eaten. She's got one left, all golden like the buddha. Natalie only has one watch, gold so she says, but the day I asked her to lend it to me for a minute to see if it looked pretty on me she yelled and screamed and I got punished. Mummy thought I wanted to steal Natalie's watch. I'd never have done that. Thi Ba always used to say I must never touch Natalie's things because she has the evil eye, so it was silly of me anyway to want to put her watch on. I'm very glad Natalie has never seen my soldier. She might have brought him bad luck and he would have got killed like the others.

Another thing that brings bad luck is when you're talkative. It's because you might say things people don't like. I'm very talkative. I have words parading through my head the whole time. This is a hidden fault because Laurences aren't allowed to talk, but it's something that makes you very unhappy, a hidden fault.

When I was little, Natalie had a rabbit in a cage in the garden. A really beautiful rabbit, all white with red eyes. That rabbit and I were very good friends, and I used to go and say my words to him. Then one day he disappeared. I think someone must have stolen him for food. It made me feel very sad.

No one has stolen the peacock for food. He's still there and I'm very scared of him because he attacks people's eyes, especially mine. Thi Ba said it was because my eyes are so pale. Daddy never goes into the garden, and Mummy and Natalie have dark eyes. Thi Ba used to forbid me to go into the garden without her, because of that horrible beast, but Mummy says it's no problem, all I have to do is be careful. Anyway I don't want to go and say my words, even if I'm being careful, to an animal that only wants one thing which is to peck out my eyes. Thi Ba hated the peacock. Once she even had an argument with Mummy, saying she couldn't understand how they could keep a peacock in the garden when they had a child with such pale eyes. Mummy got very very angry. She shouted that it was absolutely beautiful, it was part of the decor and it would stay.

My problem is that I'm not part of the decor. Except in the street, and even then not everywhere. Only on my bits of pavement. There I'm safe. Yesterday I noticed it again. One of my feet was bleeding. My own fault, as usual. I'd taken a big knife from the kitchen to defend myself against the peacock if it attacked me. I really wanted to go into the garden. The knife slipped out of my hand and went into my right foot. I had a lot of difficulty getting it out. The trouble was this happened in the hallway and I put blood on the marble. I washed the knife and put it back in its place, but however much I wiped the floor my foot made it all messy again. So I ran away before I got scolded. I went to sit on my bit of pavement where I used to sit before I met my soldier, and straight away a yellow lady dressed in black, with a mouth that went sideways, came up and put a liquid that hurt on my foot and after a bit it stopped making a mess. It was so nice of the lady that I woke up several times that night thinking of her. When I got back home I wasn't even told off for the blood on the floor. One of the servants must have cleaned it up, you couldn't see it any more. I only hope my stupidity didn't spoil the knife.

I'd very much like a knife of my own. A knife is always useful, what with all the people and animals ready to attack you everywhere. Perhaps if my soldier takes me away with him, he'll give me one. He must have lots of knives to fight with, and if he's rich maybe he's got one he doesn't want.

I wonder whether the peacock would dare attack my soldier. I don't think so, I'm sure that even the Makoui would hesitate, because my soldier knows how to fight. He's a brave dragon, a royal tiger.

Later on, if I manage to have the life I dream of, I'll have a big house all to myself, with taps and a garden without a peacock, a pool I know how to swim in, a rabbit I can talk to and marble on the floor which I can put blood on without worrying. Thi Ba, my soldier and I will live in it, in a real Nirvana, under the protection of the Hiroshima dragon, and every day we'll go to the pagoda to admire the buddha and thank him. And of course we'll have the bep with us, and he'll make us lots of delicious food and we'll all eat as much as we want. There will be nems, ban cuon, moon cakes, stuffed rice cakes, chicken with citronella, and even things that I've never eaten but which Thi Ba told me about and I've forgotten the names of. And then of course as much chocolate as we want. Perhaps Kao will be with us, if Thi Ba wants to keep him – unless she prefers her fisherman from Do Sohn who she had to leave, a long time ago, because Mummy refused to take him on as a houseboy, saying that a fisherman would never be able to serve in the house. Thi Ba cried and cried, but Mummy doesn't care when you cry, unless it's Natalie and Natalie hardly ever cries.

I remember just once at Christmas, an old sort of Christmas, when Natalie cried because she only got four dolls, very big beautiful dolls with eyes that moved, clothes as pretty as Mummy's, and real hair. At first I didn't understand why Natalie was crying, since the dolls were so marvellous you'd have thought they were dolls for buddha, but it was because she wanted the others as well, all the other ones she'd seen in the shops. Natalie screamed and stamped on her presents (her other presents, not the dolls) and shouted: 'Where are the other dolls? All the other ones!

I want them!' Mummy was devastated, like people who cry for the dead in the pagoda; she tried to comfort her but there was nothing to be done, Natalie was furious. She took those beautiful dolls and she threw them out of the window and the whole Christmas was miserable. And I was so sad, not for Natalie or for Mummy but for those dolls who were so pretty and who no one wanted. I'd have loved to make them happy, but I wasn't allowed to touch them and Mummy shut them up in a cupboard. The problem is that what's too good for me isn't good enough for Natalie, and that means no one's ever happy.

Being happy is difficult. Thi Ba used to say it isn't for people like me and her, it's for whites like Mummy and Natalie. But I'm sure I'll manage it all the same. I've already been happy, lots of times.

After all, you just have to wait for feeling sad to go away, like when you wait for a pain in your body to go away. Feeling hurt is a kind of Makoui of your own. You have to chase it away, shouting 'Dive!' very loudly. If Mummy spoke Annamese that's perhaps what she'd say to me when I'm unwanted as far as she's concerned.

But I don't care. I'll find Thi Ba and my soldier and we'll go and live in a rich house at Do Sohn, because there's the sea at Do Sohn, and it's even more beautiful than Hanoi.

I'm hungry. This boat is very big and full of food. I'd like to steal some oranges. There are lots of them, whole crates full. The men on the boat, the sailors, don't want us to have any.

The oranges are going rotten and they're throwing them in the sea.

The sailors eat chocolate. Whole bars of it. Once I asked a sailor who looked nicer than the rest if he could give me a bit. He burst out laughing and slapped me. He said: 'Piss off, you filthy little colonialist bitch. You made a pile out of the rubber when you had the chance. I hope you croak, you and all your lot.'

I've never seen rubber.

Natalie says we mustn't speak to the sailors. They hate us. It's because they're real French people and we're not.

I don't understand anything any more.

In Hanoi the Indochinese wanted to kill us: we were filthy whites, French people. Now the French say we're not French any more. Will they want to kill us too? If so, why are we going to France?

I've found out that real French people, the ones who live in France, aren't nice except when they're soldiers.

On the first boat, when we began our journey, there were some soldiers and they were all nice. The boat was marvellous too. It was an aircraft carrier, the *Bearn*. They told me that was the name of a bit of France. There were planes on it which came and went.

We got on to the boat, Natalie, Mummy and me, with

loads of other mothers and lots of other children. Daddy stayed in Hanoi; he wasn't allowed to come with us.

I'd never been on a boat. It was good fun. They put us all together in the bottom of the boat and at night we slept in hammocks, hung up like in a garden. It was hot, but I liked swinging in the air in time with the sea. During the day we could go and play on the deck, except when a plane was going out or coming back.

Then the soldiers said they were going to give a tea party for the children. Natalie knew what that was, because she'd had one before, but I had to wait and see.

It was such a long time to wait. I took off my sandals so that I wouldn't make any noise and I managed to tiptoe all the way to the kitchens. There was such a good smell I wanted to eat it. There were men, too, with enormous white overalls. They were making food.

They didn't see me. I'd only opened the door a crack, just enough to see out of the corner of my eye. They were talking about us, the children from Hanoi. We were poor little mites, they were saying. Not so much children, one of them said, more like skeletons.

That was stupid. You have to be dead to be a skeleton, and nobody had killed us yet.

Then we had the tea party. It was on a vast table, completely covered with strange cakes. And we were allowed to eat as much as we wanted. Someone gave me a cake called a nun which was a fat ball iced with chocolate, with a smaller ball on top of it, also iced. I bit into the little ball and loads of chocolate ran out into my mouth and on to my fingers. It was so good I couldn't believe it was real. I thought of Natalie, who dreams every night she's biting into a pat of butter. I've never seen butter, but perhaps it's like that.

Afterwards, I was allowed to eat another nun without even asking. And I drank some orangeade.

That evening I was ill and vomited. The ship's doctor came to see me and apparently I had caught a disease called indigestion. It's when you eat too much. I would never have believed it possible, to eat too much, until it happened to me.

I'm sad because in Saigon we were made to change boats. This one is called the *Maréchal-Joffre*. It's a merchant ship, without any soldiers on it. That's why they're so horrible.

Yesterday a little boy died. He was four years old. His mother screamed insults at the sailors. She shouted that her son had died of hunger and that all the sailors were murderers.

He couldn't have died of hunger because they give us something to eat twice a day. You're still hungry when you've finished, but only a little, not really. Not more than in Hanoi. And even if you pray to buddha very hard you can't have any more to eat. If they gave us more, the sailors wouldn't have such fun throwing food into the sea.

Thi Ba used to tell me that the buddha was all-powerful. But now I'm seven years old and I know that's not true. Even Cakya Mouni, the greatest of all the buddhas, is nothing compared to a soldier.

A soldier really is all-powerful. He can do anything. He has a uniform for parading and being applauded, a revolver and some knives to kill you with if he wants, and more food than he needs, that he can give away if he feels like it. A soldier is a real buddha. You live or you die thanks to him. Besides, there are monuments to dead soldiers and people go and pray in front of them, just like for the buddha.

I don't know where my own soldier is. He never came

back to find me on my bit of pavement. He didn't have time, or he forgot about me, or he went away somewhere else. I'm so sorry Mummy tore up the piece of paper with his address on it. I could have kept it until I learned to read. I've managed not to spend the piastres I stole for him, so when I get to France I'll be able to buy him a present. And then I'll go to Strasbourg and see if I can find him. Perhaps there is the sea at Strasbourg, like at Do Sohn. I'd love that. Maybe with those boats I like, I've forgotten what they're called, those little boats with sails. I've never been in one, but with luck my soldier will take me in one with him, I'm sure he could.

What can you find to buy in France? I've no idea and nobody will tell me. Apparently they don't even eat rice there. Anyway, on this French boat there isn't any. How can people live without rice?

A very long time ago, the world was still wild and people only had meat to eat. Animals ate each other too. Horrible cries rose up to heaven and at the same time the whole world was hungry. The screams and groans went on day and night and there was such a racket that one evening the Emperor of Heaven decided he'd had enough. 'Life isn't worth living in heaven with all this noise,' he complained, 'and anyway if this goes on much longer there won't be a man or an animal left on earth. Something must be done.'

He pondered for days and days and finally he found the solution – he would sow grass and rice over the whole earth.

The genie Kim Quang was entrusted with the task. The genie was very pleased: for years he'd dreamed of going to earth for a holiday.

The Emperor of Heaven supplied him with a sack of rice

55

and five sacks of grass seed, and ordered him: 'Plant the rice first, and only plant the grass seed afterwards. Otherwise you'll be punished.'

The genie took the sacks and flew off to earth. It took him so long to get there that he forgot the Emperor of Heaven's orders. He started by having a good rest and enjoying himself. Then he sowed the grass seed. And – horror – the grass grew so quickly and covered the ground so completely that there was no room left for the rice. In his celestial palace the Emperor of Heaven learned of the catastrophe. He threw himself into a terrible rage, which made even more noise than the moans of the people and the animals. As a punishment he turned the genie Kim Quang into a buffalo, and condemned him to eat the grass without stopping, for ever and ever, to make some space for the rice. And poor Kim Quang couldn't change back into a genie until the day when there was hardly any grass left on earth. But every day the grass grows and the buffalo has to keep on eating it so that rice can exist.

Thi Ba forgot to tell me who sowed the rice in the end. I suppose the Emperor of Heaven sent somebody else.

Rice is so important. People must be awfully hungry in a country with no rice! It's terrifying to think of.

That's probably why the real French people are so horrible: Thi Ba said that if a person doesn't have their bowl of rice every day they turn nasty. It's true the French have got oranges instead, but although oranges are good fun they're not nourishing. They're not worth as much as rice. Who'd swap their bowl of rice for an orange? No one. Do French soldiers have oranges too? I don't think so, otherwise they wouldn't be strong enough to fight. They must be given rice. Perhaps that's why they're nicer.

You couldn't be happy in a country without rice. I think

that's why Mummy and Daddy left France and came to live in Indochina.

What if they don't have water-sellers in France either? It must be a very poor country, and difficult to live in.

If I find my soldier in Strasbourg, I'll explain to him that we shouldn't stay in France, that he should bring me back to Hanoi, or to Do Sohn. We'll take his tank, put it on a boat instead of one of the planes, and there we are.

I know there's war in Indochina and not in France, but he's a soldier and he won't mind about war, it's his life. He must even like it. As for me, I'm used to it. It's no worse than dying from a disease, or for no reason at all. Anyhow, war doesn't last for ever. It'll stop when the yellow people have won.

Before my soldier, I longed for the whites to lose the war and for them all to go away to France without me. I'd have liked to be the only white person in Indochina. Since my soldier, I'm not sure any more. It's very mixed up in my mind. I suppose he must want to win the war, that would be normal, but it's a great problem for me that his happiness doesn't lie in the same direction as Thi Ba's happiness. And where does my happiness lie, in all this? Not in France, I'm sure of that.

Apparently there are no yellow people in France. I'm not surprised, if there isn't any rice. 'They very clever,' Thi Ba used to say. You'd have to be white to live in a country without rice.

There aren't any yellow people on the boat either, apart from one lady who is half yellow. Her father was French, and her mother a con gaï, according to Mummy. It doesn't bother me if her mother was a con gaï, just the opposite. Thi Ba was a con gaï before she came to the house. But all the whites on the boat refuse to talk to her and say nasty things about her, whispering behind their hands. This half-yellow lady has a stomach as big as the buddha's. She's expecting a baby. But she is terribly pretty, much prettier than all the white women. She has a real yellow skin, long thick black hair, a face like a doll and pale eyes which are almost green. Not as green as my soldier's, but they almost look it when the sun is in her face. I love the look of that lady and I love watching her.

I was stupid enough to tell Mummy I thought she was pretty and Mummy got angry: 'That filthy halfbreed, I bet she hasn't got a drop of white blood in her: I expect her mother was the bep's girlfriend and managed to fool some poor Frenchman into believing the child was his. Anyway, halfbreed or not, like all Asiatics she looks like a monkey, with that low forehead and squashed-in nose.'

I didn't understand what the bep was doing in this story. Everyone has a bep, but the only thing a bep does is the cooking. And I've never seen monkeys, but if they're like this lady they must be wonderfully pretty. I didn't answer, there's no point, but I looked carefully at Mummy. It's true her forehead is much higher, and her nose is much bigger too, and beaky instead of snubby, but that doesn't seem at all pretty to me, I don't know why.

Later, I looked at myself in the mirror in the boat's toilet and I saw that I've got a high forehead too, but my nose points up in the air like the halfbreed's nose. A bit less, but only a bit.

Mummy always says that she is a classic beauty. What does that mean, classic? Probably a rare kind of beauty that you don't find anywhere, like the peacock, or perhaps it's a French kind of beauty. Mummy sighs because Natalie isn't a classic beauty and that upsets her. Of course, she says that Natalie is very pretty, but that's not the same as a classic beauty, it's not so good.

Natalie doesn't look like me at all, but one comfort is that she has the same nose as me. So when Mummy complains about my looks she never mentions my nose.

I've never seen so much of Mummy and Natalie as I have since we've been on this boat. We're together much too much; Mummy even eats with us and I have to behave myself the whole time. It's extremely tiring; you have to think about it all the time to manage it even occasionally. I've got used to the knife and fork, but I still don't like them. It was much better with Thi Ba when I ate partly with my fingers and partly with chopsticks.

Mummy doesn't know how to eat with chopsticks. She's never wanted to try. It isn't good enough for her. It must be like walking with bare feet.

I'm not allowed to go barefoot any more. Mummy watches me all day long to see if I've got my sandals on. It makes me sad, all this extra leather on my feet. But when I feel really sad I tell myself that I'm alive, which is a piece of luck, and that makes me feel better straight away. I'm sure the half-yellow lady thinks the same.

I'd very much like to talk to that pretty lady, but I don't know what to say to her. It's difficult because I don't think I'd be able to lie to her. I like her too much. I never lied to Thi Ba, or to my soldier, but I promised Thi Ba always to lie when it was necessary and I don't know if she'd be pleased that I told the truth to my soldier.

Thi Ba used to explain that the crab has a shell to protect it, but people only have lies. And the more fragile people are, the more they must lie. She used to say I was very fragile and that I must lie a lot to protect myself. If not, people would hurt me, especially white people.

59

I lie as often as I can, but lying to my soldier would have been like lying to buddha. You mustn't lie to buddha. And anyway, why should you? He loves you as you are. White people never love you as you are: their only thought is to make you become what they want you to be.

I don't know whether or not Thi Ba loved me, she never told me, but she never tried to make me into what Mummy wanted me to be. Mummy says I must always obey white people and do everything they ask. I hate obeying, but sometimes it's even harder than usual. There are some white people I can't stand.

Thi Ba used to say the more important a white person is, the more difficult they are. I don't know if Daddy is difficult, but he's a very important gentleman because he makes electricity in the factory at the bottom of the garden, on the side where there isn't a big iron fence. It's a place where Natalie and I aren't allowed to go, so that we don't bother anyone, but where there are lots of people, yellow people mostly, but whites too. Mummy could have gone in there if she wanted, but she wasn't interested. She preferred to stay in the house, stretched out on the beige sofa in her private sitting room, reading books that came from France. Natalie wasn't interested either, she has absolutely no curiosity, but I was dying to look around.

When the Japanese were there, Thi Ba explained to me that our house was very dangerous because of the electricity in the factory. That's why there were so many bombs around our area. If the Japanese had been able to destroy the artificial light at night no one could have seen them in the dark and they'd have been able to kill everyone without being noticed.

One day I asked Thi Ba if I could go and see Daddy in the place where he worked. She started to say a load of things in Annamese. I didn't understand any of it, except that I was forbidden to go.

I listened to Thi Ba, and I stayed put.

After Thi Ba went away, I used to watch the factory a lot. There were no more Japanese, no more bombs, everything was peaceful. Thanks to the Hiroshima dragon, we hadn't even gone to the concentration camps; we were alive.

I really had no reason to make trouble when everything was going so well, but I did.

After the afternoon rest, one evening when I missed Thi Ba more than usual, I decided to go and see Daddy in his special place. I took a lot of trouble to make a good impression. I did my hair with Mummy's comb and I tied it up with the ribbons that Thi Ba used to put on me from time to time to make me look prettier. Then I put my sandals on, after washing them under the tap.

I walked up to the factory as if it was a normal thing to do, and at the entrance to the big building there was a yellow man with glasses with gold wire around them. He smiled at me without hesitation and said, 'Hello, Laurence.'

As if he knew me. I was really surprised, but then I realised that Thi Ba must have talked about me, and I replied very politely, 'Hello, sir,' smiling like you are supposed to.

He spat out his betel, to show that he was well brought up too and wouldn't talk with his mouth full. He asked, 'Have you come to see your daddy?'

I said yes and he opened the door for me. I walked into the factory and the door closed behind me suddenly, so suddenly that I didn't have time to ask where I could find Daddy.

Inside there was a bearded white man who was making

his forehead sweat into a big checked handkerchief, sitting at a table reading. He looked at me with an annoyed expression and growled, 'What do you want?'

I felt he was looking at me as if I was a barefoot con gaï, and I looked down at my dress to see if it really looked as poor as that. But it was my best dress and it wasn't even crumpled, so I didn't know what to say next, especially since I knew I wasn't meant to be there. I didn't dare mention Daddy, so I just stammered, 'I'd like to look around the factory.'

He didn't like that. He got to his feet and he growled much more loudly, 'And what else, I'd like to know? My God, you've got a cheek!'

At that moment, another white person came in through a big double door which opened in the middle. He looked at me in the same way as the first man and I realised I'd been wrong to come. But he didn't speak to me, he just said, 'Who's this?' to the first man.

The sweating bearded one stuffed his handkerchief back into his pocket and raised his arms towards the ceiling. 'How should I know? Nobody; I mean just some kid that idiot Kim let in who thinks she's going to look around the factory!'

For white people, as soon as you're not somebody important you're nobody at all; Thi Ba always told me that and it's really true.

The man who had just come in started to laugh. 'These white trash kids have got a nerve! Oh well – just chuck her out.'

'Yes, sir,' said the bearded man, in the same voice the number one boy uses when he answers Mummy. He got up from the table and started to shove me towards the door I'd come in by, but the other man got cross.

'No, no,' he said. 'Not into the director's garden!'

'Oh no, of course not, so sorry,' the bearded one stammered, and he pulled me by the arm towards the other side of the room. He opened another door and I found myself in the street. I started to walk in no special direction, thinking hard. I was furious with myself for doing something so stupid. After I'd gone the two whites would certainly have got hold of the yellow man at the door, because he'd let me in, and by now they must have found out I was the director's daughter. Then they would have gone straight to tell Daddy everything, how I'd come in spite of not being allowed to and how they'd had to send me away. Daddy must be furious. He wouldn't say anything to me himself, but he'd complain to Mummy and she'd make a huge scene and I'd be punished.

I walked for a long long time, still thinking, and it got late, probably almost dinnertime, and less hot. My feet weren't sticking to the pavement any more. I felt so fed up with all my problems with Mummy that in the end I said 'Thoï,' just like that, in my head. It would be better if I never went home again and if I learned to live on my own.

It was a good time to leave because it was cool, but apart from that it was a bad decision. I'd have done better to go just after dinner, with a full stomach. I wondered what I would have had for dinner if I'd gone back to the house, but in any case I'd certainly have been punished so I wasn't really missing anything. In Thi Ba's time, I ate what she did and I might have got a pho, or a bowl of rice with some nuoc-mâm, and with a bit of luck some lumps of food in it too. Since Thi Ba went away, though, I haven't been eating Indochinese food; I've been having what the bep makes for the whites and it's much less good. The sweet potatoes are made into chips and the rice is served without

63

any nuoc-mâm but with little bits of omelette, or sometimes a whole fried egg, or a bit of chicken as big as my finger. Sometimes there is fruit instead: a slice of papaya from the garden, or half a mango, or some lychees. Once we even had a piece of duck that wasn't glazed but peculiarly cooked in soup, like pho.

But I soon realised it was silly to think about all that because I would never have anything to eat in that house again.

I began to wonder where I could steal some food, and where I could hide for the night. I'm terribly frightened at night, what with the Makouis who are everywhere and who think about nothing else but hurting people. In the daytime they disappear, they go and have their sleep, but at night they're here.

If only Thi Ba hadn't gone away, I would have gone to her and been safe there; she'd have fed me and hidden me in the servants' house. It would have been a good solution because neither Daddy or Natalie or especially Mummy ever goes there, but I couldn't hide there without Thi Ba. The other servants would send me away, the bep especially, so as not to have any scenes with Mummy and so they wouldn't have to give me a bit of their food.

After thinking for a long time, I decided the only place I'd be safe was the pagoda. I was pleased with that idea, because apart from the pavements that's the place I like best.

I turned back because I was going in the wrong direction: I'd started walking any old way. I went towards the pagoda, walking slowly because my legs were terribly tired and I could hardly breathe.

I'd never been into the pagoda so late and I was afraid it'd be shut, or there wouldn't be any room, but no, quite the opposite, it was wonderful. There was hardly anyone there, everyone was probably at home eating their supper, and I got a mat all to myself. I was so tired I forgot about being hungry. I lay down on the mat, which was a really good one, only a little bit torn, and I fell asleep.

Of course, I dreamed about the dragon again; he follows me everywhere. He was even bigger than usual and I was trying to fight him off with a qué tam, but what could I do with a silly little piece of wood which is only useful for picking your teeth during meals? It made the dragon laugh to see that I had nothing else to protect myself with, and his laughter was so vast that the earth shook and formed into the shapes of great waves.

I was so scared that I woke up with a jump. It was completely dark and my heart was thumping hard.

I looked around me, but it was too dark to see anything clearly. There could have been Makouis all around, except if they're not allowed into the pagoda, but I'd forgotten to ask Thi Ba that and I didn't know. And now nobody would tell me the answer. All my questions are like me, unwanted.

I stayed in the pagoda, sitting with my legs folded underneath me, afraid to go to sleep again. I didn't dare move any more. I was scared in front, and on both sides, but most of all at my back. Someone could have killed me without my seeing them. It's terribly difficult to stay alive. Being asleep is the most dangerous thing, because anything can happen to you then.

I wondered what it had been like at home when they waited for me at dinnertime and I didn't come back.

I imagined Mummy being terrifically angry with me, but Natalie must have been pleased. She would have eaten my share, of course. Whenever Mummy manages to find something extra to eat, she hides it and gives it to Natalie on the quiet. Yet at meals Natalie gets given more anyway, because she is bigger and therefore she needs more food. So if I'm not there it will suit everyone.

What annoyed me about all this was not the meal I'd already missed, but all the meals to come. How was I going to manage?

I had several stolen piastres saved up, but they were for my soldier, and anyway I didn't have them on me. They were hidden in my bedroom and I couldn't see how I could get them back. There was nobody I could ask to get them for me.

Even if I'd had the piastres with me they were probably not enough to buy much food. I'm not very good at managing money. I never knew whether what I stole was worth the trouble or not. Before, Thi Ba used to count the coins and the notes for me, but since she went I don't know how to do it.

I always pretend. I say 'bâ gnu?' to the street seller but I don't understand the price he tells me. So I just hold out my hand with all my piastres in it, and he gives me as much as I can pay for. I don't worry; he never cheats me. Thi Ba used to say that yellow people never steal from children. Even Japanese yellow people. My problem will come later on, when I'm grown up. I really must find someone to teach me how to count money.

In the meantime I had to live. And since I was a white person that wasn't easy.

There are lots of children who work in return for their food, and I'd have liked to do that, I could have helped the water-seller for instance, but they're always yellow children. White children get fed for nothing, but only in their own homes, and if they haven't got a home any more they get shut up with other children who are all alone and then they're in prison, they can't leave. I had to avoid that, getting caught and shut up . . .

The night is always longer than the day. I waited so long that my whole body hurt. I couldn't unfold my legs any more, or move them at all. When the light came the noises came back too, with people talking very loudly in the street. Words are always louder in the daytime than at night, and I could also hear the horns of cars and bicycles. It was reassuring to know all that life had escaped the Makouis.

But the more time went by, the more hungry I got. My stomach was making a lot of noise too. It was complaining. Unfortunately there's nothing to eat in pagodas and I was sure that outside it would be the same. I had a sudden memory of zor, a food that disappeared so long ago I'd forgotten about it, and the taste even came back into my mouth.

It wasn't so bad, though. I was alive. Everything had gone well. I didn't see what I was worrying about. After all, nobody had ever hurt me. I was in one piece, not broken at all. I was hungry, that was all, but everybody was hungry, except really rich people.

Only now that I'd managed to stay alive, I had to manage to eat. And I couldn't see any other way except to go back to the house. There at least I was sure I'd get given food. They'd punish me for a meal or two, perhaps, but not more. The great thing was to be patient. Outside I didn't stand a chance. I was free, true, but freedom isn't much use when you're really hungry.

I got up and left the pagoda. I looked up at the early morning sun, the one who is a friend and who never hurts you, and I smiled at him. He's lucky, he hasn't got a stomach. A stomach is an awful nuisance.

I pulled at my dress, which had got all twisted up around

67

me, to straighten it out, and I made up my mind to walk as proudly as if I had a full belly. I thought it would be easy, but it wasn't very. The terrible thing, when you're hungry, is people eating in the street. Food hurts less when you can't see it.

As I'd predicted, when I got back to the house Mummy made a great scene because I'd been out all night. But that was all. After she had ranted on for quite a while, she gave me my dinner which she'd kept for me from the day before. I was a bit ashamed of thinking she'd have given it to Natalie, but in the end I felt pleased I'd come home.

Just when I started to swallow my dinner-breakfast under Mummy's furious gaze, Daddy rushed into the dining room. At first I was very scared, because I thought he'd come to scold me and punish me, but not at all. He'd only come to tell Mummy that he wasn't sure he'd be back for lunch: one of the engineers in the factory, a white, had gone crazy and was threatening to kill everyone.

White people's madness is very worrying. At Do Sohn Thi Ba's fisherman friend told us about some whites who were so mad that they paid to go fishing. Fishing is difficult and tiring, it can be dangerous, but's it's a way of getting food and earning a few piastres. No yellow person would go fishing just for pleasure. But there are rich white men who pay more than the usual price of the fish in the market to go and get it out of the water themselves. Those men made Thi Ba's fisherman friend feel very scared. He believed that a calm madman could turn dangerous at any moment, and in the way of danger the sea itself was quite enough for him.

On this boat, too, there's a tall white lady dressed all in black who seems very peculiar. She spends her time telling stories nobody can understand a word of. She grabs people as they go past, gripping their arm so they're forced to stand and listen. She even made a bruise on my arm. Apparently it was the bombs that broke her brain.

But it's not fair of me only to think about mad white people. I know perfectly well there are yellow people who are cracked too. It's hard to be fair because your heart always pulls you one way or the other, not necessarily the right way. Thi Ba used to say justice doesn't exist, and everybody has to get by as best they can. She'd say to me: 'There are people who attack, people who defend themselves, and the rest. You're one of the rest, so tell lies, it's your only protection.' Then she'd say: 'Children can only be strong when they are loved . . . My poor baby . . .' And then she'd laugh, every time she talked like that, she'd laugh very loudly and she'd end up with a serious face: 'Just you wait, my little one, just be patient. In a few years you'll still be just as pretty, and you'll see, they'll be the ones who are crying, not you.'

I remember very clearly the words she used but I don't see why I should make people cry later on. I don't want to. What I want is to make the people I love happy and for the rest to get on without me. There aren't very many of them, the people I love. Only Thi Ba and my soldier. But they're so far away in my life and in the world it's as if they were stars that I can't even see because they're so distant. Apparently there are stars like that: they exist, but nobody can see them, unless they have a special instrument like Daddy's. Even if I had Daddy's instrument, though, I wouldn't know which way to look for Thi Ba and my soldier and I could spend all my time gazing in the wrong direction.

CHAPTER FOUR

I've had scabies. By the end of the boat journey I was scratching myself furiously every night. No one would come anywhere near me, and Mummy forbade me to go near Natalie. But I wasn't the only one with the disease, and in the end we all got together in a corner of the hold. In the daytime we didn't dare move, except to go and have a pee. We went to have our meals, of course, but after all the others had finished. It wasn't bad, we had much more room. And I could eat any way I liked, nobody said anything to me. The best part was the nights. Very late, when the decks were empty of all signs of life, we went out to breathe the wind and look at the stars. Only as the boat went on, we felt colder and colder.

One chilly, rainy morning we arrived in France. In a huge great town called Marseilles. I felt scared when I looked down at the dark, still crowd on the quayside. Nobody was sitting on the ground and everybody was wearing shoes. There wasn't a single yellow person. These were the French. After a few minutes the boat came close and there were a few who started to shout:

'Bugger off, you filthy colonialists!'

Some even got stones and started to throw them at the boat. The stones bounced off and fell into the water. Until that day I'd always thought only yellow people threw stones and Mummy used to say it was because they were savages. White people must be savages too since they do the same thing.

There was a lady waiting for us, a sister of Mummy's, Aunt Simone, a funny-looking person with a black hat and thick soles on her shoes. She looked like Mummy except she was taller and had more folds on her face.

'Charlotte, my God!' the lady shrieked when she saw us.

Mummy burst into tears on her sister's shoulder. From the back, Mummy looked all funny; she seemed so thin and lost in her blue dress, like a doll made out of a toothpick.

Then my aunt kissed Natalie, but when it was my turn Mummy said: 'Oh no, not Laurence, she's got scabies!'

Aunt Simone took a quick step backwards and put up her hands: 'How horrible!' she shrieked. 'My God, how horrible! Scabies!'

'I know,' Mummy said, 'she caught it on the boat. I couldn't do a thing. And she wasn't the only one. They said we were being repatriated and so they made us travel in the most revolting conditions. Oh, the French have been awful! Luckily Natalie hasn't got it.'

My aunt took off her coat, a big black thing as thick as a carpet, and tried to make Mummy put it on. Mummy wouldn't. My aunt got cross.

'Don't be such an idiot! Anyone can see you're dying of cold! You've got practically nothing on. The three of you look as if you've just come out of Dachau, so don't catch pneumonia on top of everything else!'

I asked what country Dachau was. Apparently it was a concentration camp for real French people. But the Japanese hadn't come as far as Marseilles, it was the Germans, a sort of white Japanese, who'd done it.

In the end Mummy took the coat and wrapped it around Natalie.

Even without her coat, my aunt seemed to have a mass of clothes on: a very straight skirt, a jacket made out of the same cloth, and underneath that a jumper with a shirt that stuck out at the collar. I'd never seen anyone wear so many clothes all at once. It looked as if she was moving house with all her things on her back. Everything she wore was black because her husband had just died. But he'd died of his own accord. Worn out. Nobody had killed him.

When they're in mourning yellow people dress in white. It's much less sad. You feel bad enough when someone dies without adding to it. When someone you know disappears that's just the time when you should do happy things and wear clothes that are fun. Sadness must be looked after. But for some time now I've had the impression that whites don't know how to live.

We waited hours for the luggage to arrive, while the cold made holes in our skin. And then we got on a train and went to Nice to live with our aunt.

The apartment was tiny, with a sitting room the same size as my bedroom in Hanoi and another room which had one bed and no space around it. That was where Mummy and Natalie slept, together. My aunt and I slept in the sitting room, her on the sofa and me in a big armchair with a pouf for my feet. Apparently people in France have no space to live in. Or else it's too expensive. That's why lots of French people left and went to live somewhere else. Like my parents.

Through the window we could see the sea in the distance. It was pretty, but the weather was so cold we couldn't open the window or go for walks on the beach. I would have loved to have a coat, like the people I saw in the street, so that I could go out a bit, but Mummy had no money. She was waiting for Daddy to send her some. My aunt paid for everything. Even for me.

She was very nice, my aunt. She gave Mummy and

Natalie some of her own clothes. They were a bit too wide and a bit too long, but she made hems in them and they were wearable. Natalie was already as tall as Mummy and since she's still growing she'll end up huge. After a while I was given a knitted jacket. If I buttoned it right down to the bottom it made a sort of warm dress.

Aunt Simone looked after us the whole time. She didn't have any servants, not a single one, and she went out to buy food herself. She brought lots of good things back for us and we were allowed to eat them all. I discovered extraordinary kinds of food: butter, sausage, pâté, cheese and beefsteak. Whenever we were hungry we could just open the fridge and help ourselves. There wasn't even any point in stealing things.

My aunt bustled about the whole time, doing the house-work, the cooking, the washing up. She wouldn't let Mummy help her and made her lie down with a book to have a good rest. That's another reason why it's important to learn how to read, it means you can have a good rest. People who don't need to know how to read are the people who never have time to rest.

As soon as Mummy wanted to do something, my aunt would shout at her and Mummy would do as she said. It was incredible, I've never seen Mummy like that. She kept on and on saying 'Thank you' and 'Really, you shouldn't' and 'You're so good to us' and 'We're being such a nuisance' and 'I feel so guilty' . . . We could hardly move in the apartment; our useless suitcases (nothing in them was any good in France) stood in the hall and we had to climb over them to get from one room to the other. In the daytime it was hot because of the gas fire, but that was so expensive to run it had to be turned off at night and we froze in the darkness. I slept in my knitted dress and I scratched myself

73

all night long. I couldn't bear the wool next to my skin and I still had scabies. It was terrible: I couldn't sleep and I scratched so much I made myself bleed. Luckily scabies only comes at night.

Natalie wasn't there in the daytime: she went to school. I couldn't go because I still didn't know how to read. So Aunt Simone decided to teach me. Every day, after our afternoon rest, she gave me lessons.

I was very pleased. I thought that when I could read and write I'd be like Natalie. I'd be able to play with her, I could go to school myself, and perhaps Mummy would start to love me. I tried hard. I wanted to know everything, as quickly as possible.

Aunt Simone was pleased too. She said I worked well, I was intelligent and it was a real pleasure to teach me things. I hoped Mummy would believe her.

Now that I'm eight and I can read and write, nothing has changed.

After a time Mummy finally received some money and we went away. We got on a train and went to Paris. When we arrived at the Gare de Lyons there was another aunt waiting for us. This one wasn't a sister of Mummy's but the wife of Daddy's brother. She didn't look like anyone and she was dressed in green.

In Hanoi, green is the colour of happiness. But in any case she was so pretty, with eyes as pale as the moon and soft hair like water in ripples, I was sure she could only bring happiness.

She said I was lovely and that I was the image of Daddy. She didn't take much notice of Natalie. She kissed me and Mummy forgot to tell her I had scabies.

She took us off in a blue car that she drove herself to a little house with no garden which friends of Daddy's had lent us. It's in a part of Paris called Buttes-Chaumont where all the streets go up and down hills.

Aunt Helene settled us in. She showed Mummy how to light the boiler, then she helped us make the beds. She left after that, she was going to have dinner with friends. I was very sad. I wanted her to stay with us, but I didn't dare say so. She was the sort of aunt you don't ever imagine you could have. An aunt from Nirvana.

We didn't see her again for several days. Natalie went off to school again and I tried to help Mummy. It was difficult. Neither she nor I knew how to do anything in the house.

The first time we had to do the washing, the dye came out of some of the things and our clothes came out all different colours. I liked it better, it looked much prettier, but Mummy was furious. She claimed it was the fault of the washing powder. When we did the ironing, the materials went into lots of funny folds all over, even when we pulled them very tight to make them stay straight. The boiler kept on going out and once it almost exploded. I don't know how other mummies manage when they don't have servants, but with us, everything we ate was either burned or practically raw. The broom broke in half and the vacuum cleaner never worked at all.

At the end of the first week Mummy was in such a state that the morning she dropped a saucepan full of milk which spilled she screamed at the top of her voice and kicked the saucepan around the kitchen.

Natalie said that if it went on like that she'd leave, and, all of a sudden, Mummy burst out crying. Natalie is the only person Mummy loves enough for that to have such an effect. Luckily Aunt Helene invited us to lunch. She came to fetch us in her big blue car and took us to her house, a long way from Paris, at Le Vésinet.

75

It was a beautiful house, almost as nice as the one in Hanoi, with a park, two big Alsatians, two maids and my uncle Laurent.

My uncle is as tall and fair as Daddy, but he is very jolly, very funny and very nice. And when he looks at people, you get the impression that he really sees them.

There was lots of room in the house, but my aunt put Natalie and me at table with the grown-ups all the same, and the lunch was as good as chocolate. Afterwards I was sent outside to play with the dogs. I didn't want to; it was still just as cold in horrible old France and I had no coat. Anyway, I was scared of dogs. In Hanoi you must never go near a dog you don't know. They've often got rabies. Besides, there are very few dogs.

So I went out just for long enough to pretend I'd gone out properly and then came back as quickly as I could, on tiptoe so I didn't make any noise. That was difficult because my shoes weren't sandals, they took up so much space and they cracked when I moved. Countries where you can't go barefoot are dreadful. I sat down on the floor in the hall, by the radiator. But my aunt came out of the drawing room suddenly and wanted to know what I was doing there.

If it had been Mummy I would have lied and said I felt ill, or that my feet hurt, but this aunt was so nice I already felt I loved her. And anyway she seemed so gentle I thought she wouldn't smack me if I told her the truth. So I explained it all to her.

She didn't scold me. She kissed my hair and held me close to her body, and her perfume wrapped itself round me. She began to laugh. 'You silly little thing, why didn't you tell me?' I didn't know what to say. She went on laughing and said I couldn't come in with them because they had serious things to talk about which weren't for children. I asked why she'd let Natalie stay and she said Natalie wasn't a child any more. I said I wasn't either because I could read and write but she didn't seem to believe me and just laughed again.

She took me by the hand and led me upstairs to her bedroom which smelt like her and was just as pretty. She put the radio on and told me to have a rest and to wait there until she came back.

I would have waited for her all my life if she'd asked me to, doing nothing except thinking about her and looking at her, even when she wasn't there, inside my head where she was fixed like a picture in a book.

I took off my shoes and stretched out on the bed. It had a pink satin cover so thick that I sank into it like a pillow. It was very soft, very pleasant, and since I was tired out from scratching myself all night long I fell asleep.

When she came to wake me up, her hair falling over my face like in a dream, it was dark outside. She sat down close to me on the bed, and asked me if I'd like to stay there with her and Uncle Laurent and not live in Buttes-Chaumont any more. I said Mummy wouldn't let me, she'd already said I couldn't go when someone wanted to take me to Strasbourg. But Mummy had agreed, they'd arranged everything between them, all I had to do was say yes.

I did say yes, of course, and I stayed. I came downstairs to say goodbye to Mummy and promised I'd go and see her once a week in Paris.

Mummy explained to me in the serious voice she uses when she tells me off that she was terribly sorry to leave me there, but she was exhausted. As things were, she couldn't cope with two children at once and naturally she would keep Natalie with her since Natalie was the eldest.

When she got some money and servants again she would come and take me back, but I would be very happy here.

Aunt Helene didn't listen to a word Mummy was saying. She was squeezing me against herself, whispering in my ear that I would be her little girl and I looked so like Uncle Laurent everyone would believe I was.

Mummy and Natalie went away in the big blue car, with Uncle Laurent at the wheel, and I stayed behind.

While she was waiting for her husband to come back, Aunt Helene settled me into a very pretty bedroom where even the ceiling was covered with flowery paper. The curtains, the walls and the bedcover had flowers on them too. There was a bathroom just for me, all blue with soap the same colour and towels covered with brightly coloured boats. I hoped very much that they were boats for soldiers and not the other kind, but I didn't dare ask. Then my Aunt Helene said, in her voice which was so soft it sounded as if she was barely murmuring, that the next day she'd take me to Paris and buy me some clothes and anything else I might need.

The only thing was, it was night time by now and the scabies had started to attack me very fiercely. I tried as hard as I possibly could, but I didn't manage not to scratch. She seemed so worried that I ended up telling her everything. As she listened she walked backwards and forwards across the room, talking very loudly. It was absolute madness; why hadn't somebody done something about it before? It was very contagious and I was a walking danger.

I knew she was going to send me away and I burst into tears while I scratched and scratched.

But she kept me. The next morning she took me to the doctor and that evening, when we got back, she looked after me. She stood me in the bath with no clothes on, and she tore the skin off my whole body with a scrubbing brush. It was horribly painful, I bled all over, but I cried as quietly as I could because I hoped so much she'd keep me. Next she covered me with an ointment made of sulphur, which burned, and then wrapped me in an old sheet and put me to bed, after making me swallow a pill so that I could go to sleep.

After that we threw all my clothes away and I was cured.

For a month everything was marvellous. I got a beautiful navy blue coat with white rabbit fur on it, several skirts in different colours, some very soft jumpers and a red velvet dress with patent leather pumps. They were such pretty shoes I no longer felt at all sad about not being allowed to go barefoot. In the morning I got up late, like my aunt (I used to read in bed first, she'd brought me all the books I wanted) and then went and had breakfast in her bedroom.

My uncle left the house early in the morning and came home at night. During the day there were just the two of us.

I used to slide into her bed, which was all warm from her body and scented like her skin; the sheets she had sent from America were so soft I wanted to stroke them, and in colours most people only use for dresses. I'd sit half propped up against the pillows. Aunt Helene always kissed me tenderly and asked me if I'd slept well, and Marie, the younger and prettier of the two maids, would bring us a tray with tea and warm croissants.

After breakfast we'd read the papers. They were very thick, and full of pictures of dresses or actresses. Aunt Helene used to ask what I thought of the clothes, and sometimes she'd tear out a page and put it into a drawer in her bedside table.

Then we had our baths, each in our own bathroom. I had to wait until she'd finished doing her hair and her make-up; it took a very long time. I used to go into the drawing room, look out of the windows and draw pictures with my finger in the mist on the windowpanes.

One morning an extraordinary thing happened: everything was covered in white. It was snow. I ran outside, but at the same time I felt very scared. Snow didn't hurt, though, it squashed beneath my feet and got ugly and dirty. I ate some too; it melted in my mouth like an ice cream someone had forgotten to flavour, and just tasted of water.

It seemed very odd to me. Snow was so beautiful as long as no one touched it. Like those butterflies you have to let fly away without trying to get near them, because your fingers spoil them and destroy them.

All that's over now. I've been living at Buttes-Chaumont for a long time. My pretty blue coat has got too small, I can't wear it any more and I haven't got another. But it doesn't matter anyway, because I'm not allowed to go out, the doctor won't let me.

I've got the whooping cough and it won't go away.

I take lots of medicines, each nastier than the last. Nothing works. I cough and cough and I can't stop. The doctor says it's because I've got a heart which isn't normal. They've noticed it because of this illness but apparently I've always been like that. Until now it hasn't bothered me.

It seems that Daddy had a brother, not Uncle Laurent, another, who had the same defect. He lived in Saigon with a woman who was ten years older than him but so pretty that he loved her madly. One day, this Uncle Peter discovered that his wife was unfaithful to him. He had a dreadful fit of despair, he sobbed, he cried, and since his heart wasn't beating normally he suffocated and dropped down dead.

And his wife married another gentleman.

When I have a coughing fit I faint and fall down any old where. The first time it happened was in the street. That's why I'm no longer allowed to go out.

Since the day I got a bump on my head from the corner of the chest of drawers, Mummy has taken all the furniture out of the bedroom. There's only the bed and a carpet left.

Sometimes I faint right away and I can't breathe. They have to give me oxygen. The social workers send nurses to watch me and look after me. There are several of them and they come one after another, which means I'm never alone any more.

I'd like to chat to the nurses, but they've never got time. They just sit in a corner and read, and they only look at me when I cough.

Luckily the fainting doesn't happen very often. Perhaps once a day, not more. It doesn't come all of a sudden, only when I cough for too long and I can't stop myself. But since I've been shut up for weeks now, the time goes very slowly. For Mummy too. She complains about it. It's awful for her. She didn't love me even when I was well, so how could she love me now?

What's more, the doctor says I'll never be able to do any sports. I'll never be allowed to go riding, or skiing, or even to play with a bicycle or roller-skates. Anything which could make me fall and knock myself out is dangerous. If I went unconscious and there was nobody to bring me round I might die.

I don't care about not being able to do sports; I'd never have had the chance anyway. The tiresome thing is that I'm not normal and other people might notice. All in all I am, as Mummy says, a complete failure.

And it's Daddy's fault, Mummy claims. In her family everybody's normal.

When I first got this whooping cough, Aunt Helene, even though she'd been so nice to me, didn't want to keep me any more. She explained to me that since she went out a lot she couldn't stay at home to look after me. Mummy resents her for it. She says Aunt Helene is very rich and she could perfectly well have taken on a nurse to look after me, but she prefers to buy herself furs and jewels.

Apparently, too, if she'd really loved me she would have kept me. It was a good excuse for her to get rid of me. Children are a nuisance and no fun at all.

I'm not pretty enough or intelligent enough to be loved. Mummy often says it's a shame I look so much like Daddy. What I don't understand is that Aunt Helene said Natalie was the image of Mummy and what a disaster it was. And she couldn't see why Daddy who was so handsome had married such a plain woman.

I don't want to be loved by everybody but just by one person who will never abandon me.

I feel very sad about Aunt Helene. Sometimes at night I dream that she's changed her mind, she misses me and has come back to get me. I can smell her scent and feel the warmth of her arms around me.

I used to kiss her hard, very hard, as hard as I possibly could. I was so afraid she'd suddenly abandon me, from one minute to the next. Like Thi Ba. She used to laugh and say: 'Save a bit for tomorrow.' But I always wondered if there would be a tomorrow. I was right.

All the same, she did keep me for several weeks. She spent a lot of time with me. She took me with her to the hairdresser, to her dressmakers and to have tea with the Marquise de Sévigné. We also used to go and walk round lots of shops. In the evenings I lost her, she no longer belonged to me. I ate alone in the kitchen and they sent me to bed early. In the evenings she belonged to my uncle.

I got to be a nuisance, that was all. When I first arrived I had scabies. Not long afterwards, I got measles. I'd been to Buttes-Chaumont and Natalie, who'd caught it at school, gave it straight to me. When I had measles Aunt Helene was cross, but she looked after me very nicely. Only I was ill too long. Apparently I was anaemic, so the measles dragged on. After a fortnight, Aunt Helene had had enough. She came up less and less often to see me. She never kissed me any more at all.

When I finally got better she was very sweet to me again. She ordered a special meal with lots of desserts. Everything would have been wonderful, as before, if this whooping cough hadn't arrived almost immediately. When that happened, Aunt Helene didn't even try to look after me, she brought me straight back to Mummy. Mummy didn't want to take me back. They had a big argument but in the end Aunt Helene won. I stayed at Buttes-Chaumont. Mummy's got no choice; she has to keep me if no one wants me. I'm her daughter.

Aunt Helene has never come back to see me.

In a month's time we'll have a special meal, even if I'm not better. It'll be Christmas, and Mummy says Daddy might be here. She said that last year. He didn't come. Natalie thinks perhaps he'll stay in Hanoi for ever. He'd be right to. If I'd been able to stay I would never have come to this country. But I don't understand why we left without him. I wonder if I'll recognise him.

83

If Daddy doesn't come back, it'll still be Christmas. Mummy has promised us a big green Christmas tree up to the ceiling. I often wonder if Daddy is still alive. He never writes, or if he does Mummy never tells me. It's awful to think about that. To tell yourself that even if the Viet Minh has killed him, it'll still be Christmas in a month. We won't have a Christmas tree, or a party, and Mummy will be like Aunt Simone, all dressed in black. But it will be Christmas.

Anyway, every year there are loads of people who die before Christmas, and it's Christmas just the same for the others. Thi Ba didn't like Christmas. She used to say it was a festival for savages invented by the white buddha, the one who's a false buddha. I don't know anything about the white buddha, but I love Christmas because of the paper-chains and the shining balls. And the presents wrapped in coloured paper.

I know Thi Ba was right when she said it was something the whites invented to please themselves. But why shouldn't you invent things to make yourself happy?

I wonder whether it's possible to be happy when you're shut up without any sun. I don't think so. I'm very cross with myself because I didn't take advantage of the happiness I had. I was so happy in Hanoi, and I didn't even realise. I was outside all the time. And in the sunshine – which is a wonderful thing that doesn't exist in France. Being a bit hungry didn't matter much, it's not as bad as being without the sun. When you lose the sunshine you lose a bit of life. In France, there is a little sun from time to time, but it's so far away you can't really get warm. It just comes to say 'hello, here I am' and then it disappears again.

It's as hard as getting by without someone you love. Like Thi Ba or my soldier.

Once upon a time, very long ago, lifetimes and lifetimes

one after the other, the sun lived so close to the earth that it warmed the whole world all the time. It was wonderful. No one was ever cold and people went barefoot everywhere in the world.

Unfortunately the sun wasn't happy living so close to the earth. It saw too many things it didn't like.

One day the sun was so fed up it decided to disappear. It rushed off through the clouds and took refuge so far away that the whole world was plunged into night, a night that never ended. The people were terrified. They had only ever known daylight and suddenly they couldn't work any more, or feed themselves. Fire didn't exist then and they were dying of cold. They were starving, too, because the earth didn't produce any food. The animals couldn't find anything to eat either, and the little there was they couldn't even see.

The people moaned and cried and shouted abuse at the sky, swearing at the sun, but the cockerel was craftier. He went to find the bluebird and said to him:

'Human beings won't get anything done; they shout and yell, but that's all they know how to do. It's up to us to get the sun back, otherwise we'll all die.'

The bluebird had an idea. 'Before his last journey my grandfather told me that the sun was in love with the eastern sea. That's where we should look for it.'

They left straight away for the furthest part of the eastern sea, and there they discovered the sun hiding deep in the water. They begged it to come back, but the sun refused. It hadn't been happy with the earth, and it didn't want to try again. The bluebird started to cry, and his blue tears melted into the blue of the sea. The cockerel began to cry and his despairing cockadoodledoos rose up to the clouds. Then the sun began to ponder. I ran away because of the

85

people, it thought, but I didn't think about the animals. Why should they suffer just because human beings are so stupid?

'All right,' he told them, 'you win. I'll come back. But not all the time, and not so close. From now on I'll come every day, if you're friendly to me, but you must show me you care about me and need me. Show me you love me.'

The cockerel suggested, 'Each time I crow, you'll know that I'm thinking of you, and that you must come.'

And since then the cockerel has crowed every day at dawn to call the sun.

I haven't got a cockerel to call the sun and ask him to come and visit me in my room.

Later on, when Thi Ba and my soldier bring back the sun, we'll all three go and live near it. I'll throw my shoes into the sea and they won't even feed the fish – which proves they're useless. Fish are never mad. At least, I don't think so. One of the nurses who looks after me has a brother who is mad and they've shut him up in a special hospital. I know because one day she explained to me:

'He'll never get better. How can anyone get better when they're shut away? It's impossible. The simple fact of being shut up makes you mad. People who've been in prison a long time go funny in the head. And you, Laurence, you'd better get well quick because if you stay shut up like this much longer you'll go crackers too.'

That made me terribly scared. White people's madness terrifies me. Yellow people being mad makes me sad. But being sad is better than being frightened. I prefer yellow people's madness.

I remember when the yellow soldiers paraded in the streets of Hanoi, shouting 'Môt, Hai!' There wasn't a celebration like there was for the white soldiers – perhaps because they didn't give away anything to eat. Not a single smile or a happy wave anywhere. Along the pavements the people stood completely still, talking in very low voices; the soldiers all moved together, throwing their arms and legs forward in clothes that were too big for them. 'Môt, Hai!' As the noise reached people's ears the pavements fell silent, everyone breathed more slowly and the children stopped running about. 'Môt, Hai!' It was the war paying us a visit.

On the pavement where the water-seller had his afternoon sleep every day, there was an old man with a face so wrinkled that you could hardly see his eyes. As soon as he heard 'Môt, Hai!' he began to scream. He screamed his words of Annamese so loudly that it made him cry, and with his old body bent towards the ground he tried to raise his arms to heaven. Everybody drew back from that ong lao, as you draw back from a dead person, because they bring bad luck. Suddenly there was lots of space around him on a pavement where you could hardly move.

That poor ong lao was definitely mad, and everybody was afraid of him because of it.

What scares me the most is not war. It's two terrifying diseases: madness and leprosy. Leprosy eats the body and madness eats the brain. To be eaten before you are dead is a horrible idea.

I don't want to stay shut up here because I don't want to go mad, ever. Mad people have special doctors who torture them. They ask them lots of questions, they put them in prisons built specially, they make them all live in the same way and as the doctors want. They make them horribly unhappy for their own good. Being mad is a worse disaster than being a girl.

People run away from lepers, too, and shut them up. Maybe it's harder for them than for mad people. A mad person doesn't really know what's happening to them any more. A leper does.

I know what's happening to me. My problem is other people. I know I'm not wanted in their lives. But sometimes I wonder whether I want them in mine. Other people. 'Which other people?' Thi Ba would have said. Other people always start with your family.

Sometimes I want to scream and run away and I'm scared of going mad because I can't stand it any longer. I'll always be ill in France, I can't bear this country, I want to go home. To my pavement. To my yellow people.

CHAPTER FIVE

When I'm eighteen, old enough to go out into the world
and go to parties to meet boys, I'll make myself up to be
beautiful. I shall have fabulous dresses and I'll change them
several times a day. I shall be given quantities of jewels, all
in different colours to match my dresses. I'll do my hair in
every possible style and when I don't want to look the same
any more I'll change the colour of my hair.

When I celebrate my eighteenth birthday, Natalie, who
is six years older than me, will be jealous because she'll
already be old.

I'll have hundreds of friends. They'll ring me up and
write to me the whole time. My girlfriends will come to
tea. I shall become just like Aunt Helene. My perfume will
be the same as hers and I'll live at Le Vésinet. When I'm
eighteen, masses of men will fall in love with me. I'll see
them one by one and they'll cry when I leave them. They'll
do crazy things for me, they'll bring me flowers and they
won't even look at Natalie.

When I'm eighteen, I'll do just as I like. I'll go to parties
all year round and I'll travel everywhere in the whole world.
One day, just by chance, I'll meet my Strasbourg soldier.
I'll recognise him straight away, but he won't know me.
He'll think I'm beautiful, very beautiful, without knowing
who I am. He'll fall in love with me, he'll send me roses
and he'll come to get me in a big blue car. All of a sudden
I'll say to him: 'My name is Laurence; we once met in
Hanoi.'

When I'm eighteen, I'll go home. The war will be over
and I'll find Thi Ba. She won't recognise me either. To her

I'll seem as distant as one of those actresses you cut out of the magazines. I'll go to the pagoda with her, we'll light some incense for the buddha Cakya Mouni and I shall make her swear never to leave me again. She'll burst into tears and be sorry that she abandoned me. She'll start to love me as much as Mummy loves Natalie and she'll come and live with me.

When I'm eighteen I'll be happy.

But I've got a long time to wait. Nine years. That's as long as the whole of my life up to now.

While I'm waiting I have to go to school, learn lessons and do homework.

I've wanted to go to school for such a long time!

I used to watch Natalie leaving with her satchel under her arm. I thought she was so lucky. I was shut up in the house. I was ill.

I got better all of a sudden. Nothing new had happened; the medicines were the same, and the doctor too. Our cleaning lady said it was a miracle, because it was just before Christmas, and the first day I was allowed out of doors she took me to a white people's pagoda to light a candle.

It was the first time I'd been into a church.

Instead of the buddha there was a thin white man with a beard who'd been nailed to some planks. We had to kneel down in front of him and pray to him and thank him, just like the real buddha. The big difference is that there are benches, and you can sit down so that you get less tired. You have to kneel as well, but upright with your hands together, not bending forward to touch your forehead to the ground.

The odd thing about this white buddha is that they'd nailed him to the planks because they thought he was a false god. Then they realised that was a mistake. He was a real god. But they left him nailed to the planks just the same, instead of saying sorry and putting him right again. It must seem funny to him when people prostrate themselves in front of him without even taking his nails out.

I gave thanks to this new god for several minutes, very politely, and since you go to see him in order to get something you want, I asked him to be sent to school.

Well, there was a second miracle: I went.

Not straight away. It was the middle of the school year and the place Natalie goes didn't want to have me. They said I had to wait for the beginning of the next year. Mummy was very cross. By the time the next school year started I'd be ten, and she thought that was very old to be starting school.

So at first I stayed at home. But this time I was in good health and I could go out as much as I liked. Mummy was out all day, and Natalie had lunch in the school canteen. I was alone with Germaine, the cleaning lady. She was very nice, a bit dirty – which is not surprising because of the housework – with a big bust that moved about and very curly black hair. She had a husband who beat her very hard and who drank, so she preferred to stay at our house as long as possible. She was supposed to give me lunch and go home after that. She had nothing more to do and she wasn't paid for the time. But since she didn't like being in her own home we came to an arrangement. She didn't tell Mummy anything about what I did and I didn't say that she stayed in the house every afternoon.

When we'd finished lunch, she'd settle down in the sitting room, all nice and warm next to the radiator. She read photo-romances. I'd look for some money to steal, there was always a bit lying around somewhere, in Mummy's coat pockets or at the bottom of her handbags. I'd take a coin or two, occasionally even a note, and go out for a walk.

I used to wander around the Buttes-Chaumont park and buy some peanuts or some toasted almonds. When I'd pinched enough money I used to take the bus and go to the cinema. Or else I'd go to the café at the corner. I used to chat to the owner and his wife. They were very nice. They called me Laurence and gave me beer to drink. I adored it. If I didn't have enough money on me, they used to give me credit and I'd come back and pay them later.

That café was really lovely. It was called the Petit Bougnat and you felt at home there. More like an Indochinese home than a white home, too. I used to perch on one of the high stools and drink a half, never more. Just for a game, I'd make the froth spill over on to the bar, and the landlady would laugh and mop it up with a big sweep of her cloth.

It was a lot more pleasant than school.

But I didn't know that then.

What happened was that Daddy arrived. All of a sudden. Without any warning. I suppose he wanted to surprise us. It was one afternoon when Germaine was reading quietly in the sitting room and I was at the café. Germaine lost her head. She told Daddy everything and he sent her to fetch me.

I rushed home. We kissed each other vaguely, and didn't really know what to say except 'All right?', 'Yes, and you?', so I suggested he come with me to the Petit Bougnat for a half pint. They're full of men, those cafés, so I thought he'd be pleased, but not at all. He looked flabbergasted, said 'No thank you,' and went off to have a rest in Mummy's bedroom.

Germaine fled and I settled down to read the photo-romance she'd left behind.

When Mummy got back late that evening, to begin with she was over the moon because Daddy was home at last. But then he told her that I spent my afternoons drinking beer in a café and she made a terrific scene. I thought I was going to be punished, but it really turned out to be an unusual day. Mummy calmed down and we all went out to dinner in a restaurant.

Because there weren't any other rooms, Daddy shared Mummy's bedroom. The bed wasn't very big and they didn't get much sleep. I could hear them talking and moving about, even though Mummy kept saying, 'Don't, don't, Natalie might hear.' In the daytime Mummy was very tired. The minute she sat down she fell asleep. She slept all the more because instead of going out all day long she took to staying in.

Daddy seemed very happy. He sang to himself in the morning while he was shaving. He was on holiday and didn't have to go to work. During the day he stayed in with Mummy, reading or doing crosswords. He made a lot of telephone calls; he was looking for an apartment.

He found one very soon and we moved house.

To start with I missed Germaine and the Petit Bougnat but I just had to get used to it.

The apartment is absolutely huge. But at the moment we're putting up friends of Daddy's who've also come back from Hanoi, which means I have to sleep in the hall, and I must say I don't like it at all.

Mummy said straight away that she was very pleased she could have a room to herself again. They furnished a room for Daddy, part study and part bedroom, but he didn't seem very happy about it. He would have liked a proper bedroom, but since Natalie also wanted a room of her own he couldn't have one. Daddy and Mummy argued about this a lot. Daddy wanted to sleep in Mummy's room. She was furious. Daddy snores and stops her sleeping, so she didn't want him. Mummy snores too, but she doesn't know that.

Anyway, in a few months' time the guests will leave and we'll have two more rooms. This apartment is gigantic but with so few rooms it'd have to be rebuilt to suit us properly.

Daddy has gone back to work. He goes out with Mummy much less, he hardly ever speaks to her, and not at all to Natalie and me, and he doesn't sing in the mornings when he's shaving now. Life is back to normal.

At mealtimes, we all eat together but nobody talks to each other, we just exchange a few words to ask someone to pass the bread or something like that, because you have to be polite. Meals last hardly any time. We have a maid called Raymonde, she smells very bad but no one seems to notice.

And I go to school. Daddy found a convent that would take me in the second term so I didn't have to wait until the new year. Because of my age they put me straight into Class 8, but it's very hard. Apart from reading and writing, I don't know anything. The other girls have been at school for years and they know masses of incomprehensible things.

The first time I went to school I was so pleased. They bought me some clothes which weren't at all pretty but were brand new and the right size for me, and I also had Natalie's old satchel all to myself and a load of books. Suddenly I had lots of things of my own, all at once. Only it was spoilt straight away.

The head nun looked like a policeman dressed up as an old lady. She stared at me with a very discontented expression, as if I had to be punished. Perhaps I had to be punished because I'd come to school at the wrong time, and also because I didn't know anything. As usual, I wasn't wanted and I was a nuisance.

She called a less important nun and got rid of me. The less important nun took me into a dark room where there were lots of girls all dressed the same, and the same as me too since that morning I'd put on my special clothes, and there wasn't a bright colour anywhere, nothing but the dark blue and white of the clothes and the brown and grey of the room and its furniture. There was another nun, too, even uglier than the others, who was there to teach us what she knew. She sat me down at the very back and said:

'Since you aren't capable of following the lesson, you will copy this text.'

And then she turned her attention back to the others. I listened a little to what she was saying and it was true I didn't understand any of it, except that she had a voice which pronounced each bit of every word as if she wanted to hit it.

The text was silly; it was the story of a baby that everyone came to worship in a place built for animals. I took her my piece of paper. She took it without looking at it and put it down on her desk, still talking to the other children. So I thought I'd finished. I opened the door and walked out.

The nun ran after me, caught hold of me in the corridor and made a great scene. I should have gone back to my seat and sat still. You're never allowed to leave by yourself, you have to wait until all the others have finished, even if you have nothing more to do. It's terrible how much time you waste at school. You can't even think properly because you mustn't stop listening. And most of the time they aren't telling you anything interesting anyway.

The only kind of nuns I like are the ones you eat, the ones we had on the *Bearn*. If the nuns at my school were turned into cakes, they'd make really enormous ones that could feed loads of hungry children and they'd be much more use like that.

Another thing I can't bear at school is having to learn sentences by heart and recite them to the white god. I can't bring myself to love that god. He's too much like the whites.

In one class I stole a piece of modelling clay and made myself a tiny little buddha, all of my own, which I carry everywhere in my pocket or my satchel. At home I hide it under my bed. The trouble is it's too soft, it goes out of shape all the time and I have to remake it every day. The other trouble is it's not very beautiful. It's red and green, which it could well be, but the colours aren't pretty. I couldn't find any golden clay. There was yellow, but I loathe that. Real yellow is a violent, ugly colour. But I adore gold and buddhas are always golden. Modelling clay isn't really what you need for a buddha. Especially when you're not very good at it, like me. I'm very clumsy with my hands and it never comes out like what I have in my head.

I've given the piastres that I stole in Hanoi for my soldier to my modelling-clay buddha. There was no point in keeping them for him any longer. Nobody wants piastres in France, so I can't buy anything with that money.

Personally I feel certain buddhas don't like francs, they prefer piastres. I'm sure my little buddha is pleased with his piastres, even if he can't do anything with them. Anyhow, buddhas never spend the money they're given. For them, it's just proof that they are loved.

To get back to the school: the first day I was very miserable and then that night in bed I told myself perhaps

I was wrong, and if I tried hard everything would be all right. Since then I have been trying, but it isn't really all right. I've got the Class 8 books, but not the ones before. What's more, since the start of the year I've missed lots of things the nuns have already explained. I stole some money from Mummy's bag while she was in the bath and went in secret to buy myself a torch. With that I can try to learn the lessons hidden under the covers at the bottom of my bed. At night after dinner.

Mummy insists I go to sleep straight after the evening meal and, since I sleep in the hall, she sees if I leave the light on. And I don't really have time, in the day, to learn the little that I understand in the books. The school head said in front of me that I'd never manage it, and I should be given extra private lessons. But Mummy just shrugged and said I wasn't as stupid as I seemed. According to her, the final exams are of such a pathetically low standard that if I don't come top, let alone pass, it means I'm absolutely beyond redemption.

And anyway school is so expensive that it would be out of the question to give me private lessons as well.

I love the history book, and the geography book, the quotations and the set pieces. As for compositions, they'd be fine if you only had to tell a story, but the grammar is the most important part and I don't know how to use it. Maths is the hardest. It's full of divisions with decimal points in them and I can't even do division without. And another horror is subtraction and multiplication, when I only know how to count up to a hundred.

What upsets me the most is the other girls in the class. They laugh at me the whole time. I am the Tonkinese, the savage, and they've even nicknamed me Little Red Riding Hood because Mummy did my hair in three buns, one over

97

each ear and one at the back. I've cried and pleaded with her to stop doing my hair like that but she refused. I'm a cretin and the other girls are too, the hairdo is a work of art and I have absolutely no aesthetic sense. Mummy even took me to the Louvre one Thursday afternoon to give me a sense of beauty, but no one had a hairdo like that there. So when we got home from the museum I took some scissors and cut all my hair very short so nobody could do anything else to me. I got a good slap but that's less hard to bear and anyway it didn't last long.

The other girls acted as if I hadn't changed. They still call me Little Red Riding Hood.

The only time I get any peace and quiet is during the gym lessons. I don't do gym, the doctor said I mustn't.

The nuns have very odd ideas. Every morning when we arrive we have to say prayers in a big group. On Fridays they take us to mass and on Sundays we're supposed to go with our families. But since nobody at home goes (Mummy made me swear not to tell them) I can pretend I go without going.

It has taken me some time to get used to this new religion. To start with I used to say terrible things and I got very bad marks. The Holy Trinity is a complete mystery to me and I don't see why it was such a tragedy for Jesus to die, since he knew he was going to be resuscitated. I'd be quite happy to be dead for three days if I came back to life afterwards and suddenly everyone had to adore me for it.

I also think the story of Judas is really sad. That man Jesus would never have become such a powerful god if Judas hadn't betrayed him. Yet he knew all along what was going to happen. He could easily have stopped Judas doing such an awful thing, and saved him. But instead he made use of it. He lost Judas so he could become a god himself.

98

In my opinion Nirvana sounds much more fun than heaven. I wanted to become a buddhist like Thi Ba, but Mummy wouldn't hear of it. Apparently it's an inferior religion, only good enough for yellow people.

As far as I'm concerned, that inferior religion suits me very nicely, much better than the other one. When I see all the girls at school with crosses round their necks, it gives me a shock. If Jesus had lived much later and he'd been shot, bombed or guillotined, would they have a gun, a bomb or a guillotine made of gold hanging out of their school blouses? It's really a ridiculous religion.

I've only been going to school for three months and I've had enough. To think it's going to go on until I'm eighteen is horrifying. I don't see why you have to learn all that when you're a girl. Later on you always end up getting married and staying at home. So what's the use? It's true some women work, but Mummy says that's not done in our circle. And soon Natalie's going to find herself a husband.

When she was my age Natalie already knew Greek and Latin perfectly. In Hanoi she had a tutor who came to the house every day to teach her loads of things. But I don't care if I don't know Greek and Latin. They're useless languages, they don't help you chat to people and make friends. What I would have liked was a tutor to teach me Annamese.

Whenever I ask for something, it seems it's always stupid. Natalie always gets what she wants, or almost always. Probably because she only asks for intelligent things. She has so many clothes and other things she doesn't know where to put them. She goes out with Mummy a lot, to restaurants, to the theatre, to the cinema and to concerts. Yet she's never happy. She always wants something she hasn't got. It's hard to be happy when you want everything. Occasionally Mummy gets cross and tells Natalie off. That always turns out badly. Natalie throws a fit and screams and bites her pillow. Mummy loses her head and gives in.

Mummy says Natalie will have to find a husband who's very rich and who'll spoil her and give her everything she wants. My view is that even if Natalie has everything, it won't be enough for her. Maybe I'm wrong, but that's what Thi Ba used to say. In Hanoi, as well as her English nurse, Natalie had a little yellow girl of her own age who was her servant and followed her everywhere to do things for her. I would have loved to have someone like that; we'd have become friends and we'd have played together. But Natalie wasn't happy. She was always going to Mummy and saying the little yellow girl was no good and that she ought to be punished because she didn't look after her well enough. The little yellow girl cried and said it wasn't true. In the end Mummy sent the yellow girl away.

Thi Ba used to claim that Natalie would never be happy because she had a nature incapable of happiness. There really are people like that: very rich people who live where they want, in the way they like, and who are never satisfied.

A long time ago in Indochina, there were two brothers who were quite unalike. The elder brother complained about everything all the time. His parents gave him loads of presents but they couldn't make him happy. The younger one was only allowed to have whatever his brother didn't want, but he learned to be content with that. And then the parents died. The older brother took their lovely house and all their money and he left the younger brother with an old bit of ground and an ancient house which was falling down. The younger one didn't say anything, because older brothers have a right to everything, but he spent his days and nights rebuilding the old house, all alone.

When the house was habitable, the younger brother married a very pretty poor girl who he was in love with. Together they tried to make something grow on the old bit of land, but the land was dead and couldn't support anything. So they went to pray to buddha and asked him to help them, otherwise they'd die of hunger. The buddha took pity on them and he made a carambola tree grow on the dead land. It was only a very little one, but the younger brother and his wife took so much trouble watering it and looking after it that it grew to be a beautiful great tree with superb fruit which meant they could earn a living. But one afternoon, a strange and magnificent bird, dressed in all the colours of the rainbow, came and perched in the tree and ate all the fruit. The younger brother burst into tears at the foot of the tree.

'Oh,' he cried, 'what is going to become of my wife and me? The fruit is all gone and we shall die of hunger.'

The bird was ashamed.

'Forgive me,' he said, 'I didn't realise. But don't worry; I shall make you rich. Prepare a bag with three empans and wait for me; I shall return tomorrow.'

The next day, as good as his word, the heavenly bird appeared. During the night the younger brother and his wife had made a bag of three empans out of the young woman's dress.

The bird took the younger brother on his back and flew away across the world. He flew on for li after li, until he came to an island as brilliantly green as newborn jade.

Across the whole island were strewn pieces of gold and precious stones of all colours.

The younger brother, dazzled, chose the stones he

thought most beautiful. When the bag was full, he returned home on the bird's back.

The younger brother became very rich, immensely much richer than his older brother. When the older one realised that, he flew into a violent temper.

'How did he get hold of so much money, and why isn't it mine?' he screamed in rage. 'There must have been some treasure hidden on that rotten old bit of ground.'

So he went to see his younger brother and claimed the treasure as his own.

'Why are you getting into such a state and demanding things that aren't yours?' the younger one replied. 'You don't even know how our good fortune really came to us.'

And he told him the whole story.

When the older brother heard what had happened, he was passionately jealous.

'I want that carambola,' he demanded, quivering with anger. 'It ought to be mine, it's on that patch of ground I should never have given you.'

The younger man wasn't surprised, he knew that his brother always wanted everything, and he gave way graciously.

'Take it, if it'll make you happy; it's yours.'

For months on end the elder brother stayed by the carambola, waiting for the bird. When it didn't appear, he started complaining.

'My brother lied to me. There was hidden treasure in the ground and all the rest was just a story he made up.'

But one evening the magic bird came back and started to eat all the fruit. The elder brother rushed straight up to him, moaning, 'Oh, what have you done, you wonderful bird? My wife and I have nothing to live on but this fruit; now we'll starve to death!'

The bird comforted him immediately. 'No, no, don't worry, I'll make you rich. Make a bag with three empans in it and expect me at the same time tomorrow.'

The older brother made a bag with nine empans in it, so that he could fit more treasure inside, and with this huge sack he set off on the back of the magic bird. When they got to the island he filled his enormous bag, and he only managed to clamber back on top of the bird with a great effort. The magic bird could hardly fly. Almost crushed by the weight, he hauled himself along, barely skimming the ground. When he passed over the sea he faltered, and the older brother, dragged down by his fortune, fell into the water and drowned.

If Natalie had listened to the Indochinese she would know this story. But Natalie only listens to white people.

As for me, my head is full of stories Thi Ba told me, but they don't mean anything here in France. That's because they aren't stories made for white people.

CHAPTER SIX

She's bought a piano. A huge, hideous black thing which clutters up the sitting room and makes a lot of noise. I know they call it music, but what's the use of bad music? This piano is supposed to be for Daddy and Natalie. When it's Daddy it's bearable, but when Natalie plays, repeating the same thing over and over again and stumbling in the same places each time, it's appalling.

At first the piano didn't really bother me, apart from being so ugly and noisy. I stayed in my little corner, safe with my thoughts, and waited for it to pass.

But now something dreadful has happened: she's decided that I ought to play the piano too. A young lady from a good family must be able to play the piano – it's compulsory. I don't feel at all like a young lady of good family, you only have to see what the other girls in my class think of me . . . And what about Daddy? He's not exactly a well-brought-up young lady! As for her, she learned the piano when she was my age, but she gave it up and I quite see her point. The piano is fine for Natalie but why must I do it? She's going to make me suffer for years and years, just for something I'll give up as soon as I can. Like she did.

Learning the piano is a nightmare. It's another of those things they teach you with slaps, scoldings and punishments. Like education. If I could, I wouldn't learn anything. I wouldn't even go to school. And, as usual, I'm not made right. My hands are too small. I know they are ten-year-old's hands and they're going to grow, at least I hope so, but apparently they're too small for my size and so they're likely to be too small all my life. If I'd never been made to do the piano no one would have noticed – nobody would have looked at my hands first – but now it's a settled fact and everyone knows. I can't do the right exercises for my age. I have to choose pieces for beginners of five or six and I feel perfectly ridiculous. The worst thing of all is that the noise I make is even more awful than Natalie's racket.

You're not allowed to do what you want before you're twenty-one, unless you get married first. So I've got eleven more years of battling with this terrible instrument. If it was even a nice colour – but it looks like a coffin or hearse dumped in the middle of the sitting room. When I have my own apartment there will never be a piano in it, I swear.

Words are my great comfort. I've discovered they're absolutely blissful. I go and look in the dictionary, in secret, and I find the prettiest words. Alabaster, amble, melancholy, twilight, memory, evasion, regret, windward, verge, weeping willow, for example. Sometimes they are complicated words, I forget what they mean and I have to go and find them again. I don't like loving something without knowing what it is I love.

I also play at marrying up the words that please me. So that they aren't all alone. 'Cloudy twilight, steeped in melancholy . . .' That may not mean anything, but it makes me dream.

Sometimes I stop loving a word. For no reason. It just suddenly goes away. That worries me a little because it's not very nice for the word, but there's nothing I can do about it. You can't make yourself love, or love because you ought to. Otherwise all mothers would love their children.

What I like best is inventing words. The trouble is that you can't use them. It's not allowed. Often I forget that I've made up a word and I use it. If it's when I'm speaking, it doesn't really matter, people seldom listen to what I say.

But if I write it in an essay it causes a great scene. I'm bound to get a bad mark and since she never forgets to look in my exercise book at the end of each week I get scolded to death. It's awful not to be able to do anything without getting caught.

I've also discovered punctuation. Punctuation is great fun. The pity is that you can write it but you can't say it. With punctuation, if I'm not careful, I speak it. I say it all: the full stops, the commas, the semicolons, the dots, exclamation marks and question marks, the colons, the brackets and even the inverted commas. Obviously it sounds a bit odd, but I love it. At school they take a poor view of it, even when I'm reciting something. At home she can't stand me doing it:

'What on earth did I do to give birth to such a halfwit!'

With an exclamation mark, of course!

As for Daddy, he never says anything. True, he doesn't listen to me, even when I ask him a question. I say the same thing several times and in the end she intervenes:

'Your daughter is asking you a question, Andrew.'

Her he listens to. It's as if he suddenly wakes up, his eyes focus, and he stares at me.

'What do you want?'

Then of course I no longer feel like saying it, but I have to.

It's extremely tiring to be a little girl in a world where everything is forbidden. Between the things that 'just aren't done', although nobody can explain to you why not, and all the things which have to be done in a certain way and absolutely not in any other, there's no end to it. Not for me, anyhow. I think the other girls manage better.

I'd really like to have a friend. A person I could play with and talk to. It'd be her and no one else. I could love her, perhaps even love her a bit too much. But it seems impossible. I'm too different. I don't see quite how I'm so different, but that's the way it is and it's a disaster.

When you're different, people leave you alone. And being alone is something I don't like at all. Perhaps one day, with a bit of luck, I might get to be like the others? I said that the other day, and for once she listened to me. She started laughing.

'You poor child, you'll never manage it!'

If that's true, will I feel so lonely all my life? It's a terrifying thought.

I suppose my soldier, in Hanoi, didn't have time to realise that I was different. If they'd given me to him, he would have done the same thing as Aunt Helene, he wouldn't have kept me.

Later on, I'm never going to have a child. I'd be too frightened of having a little girl who'd be different too. And *I* wouldn't be able to teach her to be how she ought to be. I'd be incapable of educating a child. I refuse to slap anyone; I won't raise my voice even to my dolls.

I've got three dolls now. A really big family. There's Alabaster, whom Aunt Helene gave me for Christmas. She didn't come to see me but she sent her by post.

I cried a lot. From pleasure because I had Alabaster, and from sadness because Aunt Helene hadn't wanted to see me. Alabaster is my favourite. I think she's the only one I really love. I don't know if I can love several people at once.

Alabaster is blonde, with long wavy hair. She has big eyes that don't shut and very soft skin which I stroke at night when I'm falling asleep. She sleeps cuddled up to me and I talk to her with punctuation.

There's also Rivulet, who was a present from the lady

who lived here for a time with her husband when they came back from Hanoi. Rivulet is very small and dark with black eyes which close. Her head is made of porcelain and her body is made of material, apart from her hands and feet.

And then there's France, whom she bought me for my birthday. France looks terribly like Natalie, that's why I don't really love her and why I gave her as a name a word I feel indifferent about. Apparently she's the only one I gave a sensible name to.

Dolls are practical things. They don't eat, they don't move, they stay where you put them. They never cry and you can not bother about them without feeling guilty. I think there are loads of mothers who ought to have dolls instead of having children.

I would have loved to have a yellow doll, but they don't exist here.

Natalie wanted me to baptise my dolls, but I refused to do it, even for France. I loathe the white religion more and more. It might do you some good when you're dead, if you've deserved it enough, but it makes life even more difficult.

At my school we have to go to confession every week. It's compulsory. You have to tell a gentleman you've never met and who is hiding behind a piece of wood with holes in it all the bad things you've done. It seems to me like going to the house of a complete stranger and taking all your clothes off.

For a long time I was smart enough to be careful. When I saw the gentleman, I lied meticulously. I became almost perfect. Not absolutely, otherwise he wouldn't have believed me. I invented for myself two or three not very important bits and pieces and it all went fine. But they put me in such a dream with their superior religion and all that's so remarkable about it that I almost landed up believing in it. I thought to myself: 'What if I tried to believe in it? What if I tried telling the truth? Perhaps they're right, perhaps that's what you should do. If I don't try it, how will I know? And anyway, it's quite safe. The priest isn't allowed to repeat what you tell him, it stays a secret between him and you. Besides, he doesn't know you, he doesn't know who your parents are.'

So one Friday I was honest with him, instead of lying. It was hard, but I did it. I told him I was in the habit of stealing from Mummy's handbag when I needed something. That I'd always done it and that she never noticed.

At the time, the priest didn't say anything very important. He told me off a bit, but quite nicely, and then I had to say five paters and four aves. It cost a bit more, that's all.

A few days later there was a huge scene. She hit me and shouted at me.

'You're a thief, a dirty little thief! You've always rummaged in my bag, you've always taken money from me!'

The priest had told on me! She said that wasn't true, she'd noticed it herself, but she must think I'm an idiot. Between the confession and the scene with her, I hadn't stolen anything, not a thing. So? The worst bit is having to go on making my confession, every Friday. I can't get out of it. But that priest, always the same one, well hidden behind his bit of wood with holes in: I hate that priest. I'd like to see him dead. He'd go to his heaven, after all; he'd be happier, wouldn't he?

The most annoying part about this whole episode is that I daren't steal anything now. I'm afraid of getting caught. And immediately I started feeling hungry every day. I know it's not normal, and that the rest of the family who eat the same as me aren't hungry. I have a cup of tea in the morning when I wake up and I eat twice a day, at midday and at seven. I don't know how I manage it, but between the cup of tea and lunch I'm starving. And it's worse in the afternoon before dinner. It isn't normal to eat every time you're hungry, but before I used to use the money I'd stolen to buy some bread and ham or pâté on the way back from school. That's impossible now, and it's a long time to wait until the evening meal. Why am I so stupid as to feel hungry when I shouldn't? I don't know and I can't help it.

I'd also like to teach myself not to have any more nightmares. I still get chased by the Hanoi dragon, who has emigrated with us, and sometimes I dream that real French people with horrifying faces contorted with hatred make a circle around me and throw stones at me until I'm dead, shouting, 'I hope you croak, you filthy little colonialist bitch!'

Dying is very hard, even in a dream. You wake up suffocating, your heart too big for your body and beating too fast, your head full of fear, and it takes a long time to get your breath and to bring yourself back to life.

At your real death, they put you in a wooden box and bury you. I find that very disagreeable. I'd prefer to be turned into ashes and scattered over the sea, as is sometimes done. It's completely idiotic to be put into a tomb; it takes up space that living people could use and it's much better to be eaten by fish than by maggots. And anyway tombs are a bit like putting dead people in prison.

I'm terrified of going to prison one day. Since she's found out that I steal things, she keeps saying I'll end up in prison. I have terrible memories of the bed with bars they shut me up in when I was little. But even if it meant I had to sleep in that bed again, I'd still like to go back to Hanoi. To find Thi Ba.

The funny thing is, the rare moments you feel free are when you're alone. When no one is there to shout, or get angry, or hit you.

If it was someone I loved who shouted, would I be able to stand it better?

I don't know. Thi Ba was very gentle. And Aunt Helene was too.

As for me, if that Strasbourg soldier had taken me away with him, I would always have been terribly kind and gentle.

He would have taken me in his arms, he would have hugged me very very tightly and he would have said, 'I'll never shout at you, I'll never get angry with you, I promise. Even if you tell lies, even if you steal. I love you.'

I would've sat on the floor and put my head on his knee. He'd have stroked my hair. I would have shut my eyes to feel more strongly that he was close to me and I'd have known I belonged to him.

And I'd never have lied or stolen anything again. I wouldn't have needed to.

Only my soldier and I haven't got buddha's protection. Perhaps it's because Jesus, the white god, is like Mummy: he doesn't want it to happen and since I'm in his country now, he's more powerful than buddha.

A very short time before the trouble about the priest and the confession I got into some other trouble because of my soldier.

By watching what other people do, I've learned how to use the telephone. I've also discovered the directory, and since I can now read without any problem I can find whatever I want in it. So I looked up the railway stations and I asked how I could get to Strasbourg. Someone explained it all to me very nicely, repeating what I had to do.

I was so happy to know how to get to Strasbourg, at last, that I decided to find a way to go there for real. I talked it over with my modelling-clay buddha and he agreed.

I stole the money I needed, but no more than that, so it wouldn't be a real theft. It took me a long time to steal so much. Weeks and weeks. I didn't dare take too much at once, I was always afraid somebody would notice. Even when you're used to it, you still have the same fear of getting caught. It must be hard if it's your job. If I could do it another way, I'd much prefer to.

Of course, I wasn't sure I'd be able to find my soldier in Strasbourg, but in my head I told myself that if I didn't even try it'd be a way of telling him I didn't love him enough to undertake anything. I was cross with myself, too, because I'd taken so long to reach this decision. That wasn't good.

I'd had time to think about it, since Hanoi, and I knew all soldiers were put together in a special house, a barracks, and I thought that when I got to Strasbourg all I had to do was to look for that house.

On the morning when I saw I had just the right amount of money, I made myself look as beautiful as possible. I had a bath with the bath foam Aunt Helene gave me, which I was keeping for a special occasion since I knew I'd never get any more. I washed my hair, too, not with my shampoo but with Natalie's, and I even used her hair-dryer because there was no one to see me, instead of letting my hair dry in the cold. I was forced to put on my school uniform, because I haven't any other clothes, but I told myself it didn't matter because he'd be in uniform too.

After that, instead of going to school I took the metro, with a ticket I'd stolen from Daddy, and I arrived at the Gare de l'Est. It's a vast station, all black and noisy. You get lost and since I had no watch I was scared I'd be too late, but there are plenty of trains to Strasbourg all the time and when I asked a gentleman at a place marked 'Information' he told me there was no problem and all I had to do was to buy a ticket.

I joined the queue in the place you had to go, and I felt very proud of myself for managing so well on my own, but when I got to the front of my queue the gentleman dressed in grey on the other side of a window with a hole at the bottom told me it was the wrong queue, because he only sold first class tickets. I would never have dared to steal enough for first class, so I went away and stood in another queue, just beside the first. There, everything went well to begin with. The gentleman made out the ticket, then he asked me for the money and it was masses of francs, many more than I'd stolen. I was very surprised and said that on the telephone, several weeks earlier, they'd told me a different price. But the gentleman explained that the fares had just gone up. I was furious with myself for having taken so long to steal the money, or not stealing more than I needed, but it was too late and I couldn't do anything about it. With train tickets you can't bargain for a better price.

There were lots of people behind me who were getting impatient and I had to go away.

I started crying. I was sick and tired of everything, and I went and sat down on the ground in a quiet corner, a thing that's not done when you're white, and in uniform to boot, and I tried to think.

I could see I'd never get myself out of this mess if buddha didn't help me, but since he couldn't help me in France there was no future for me. I didn't know what to do with myself. I didn't even have a metro ticket to get home.

After a little while I got fed up with sitting on the ground crying, with all those people jostling me, and at the same time I remembered that at least I had plenty of money, enough to take the metro in peace and to have some left over. I looked in my pocket, but there was nothing there any more. I went back and queued at the same place to ask if I'd left the money on the counter, but the gentleman there said I hadn't.

I just had to go home on foot, asking my way as I went and changing direction all the time.

It took me almost all day, and I was so tired I didn't wait to think up an explanation for my absence. I decided to say nothing at all. It was a piece of bad luck that Mummy was there, it's always bad luck for me when she's there, and of course she started shouting at me. After a few minutes I felt so weak from standing up with all those shouts raining down on my head that I leant against the wall and started to slide slowly into a faint. Mummy stopped yelling; she picked me up and carried me to my bed, and I fell asleep all of a sudden, without knowing why.

When I woke up, Mummy was very nice. She behaved as if I hadn't done anything wrong and she's never mentioned that day again.

Sometimes I wonder why I can't bring myself to love her for real. If she only loves Natalie she must have a good reason, and I can't hold that against her. It was up to me to be better so that she could love me too. I realise Natalie has lots of qualities I'm not capable of appreciating, and that in any case I could never be as good as her.

But there's something odd that happens in my mind. However well I know that Mummy and Natalie are much better than me, I have absolutely no wish to be like them. Mummy talks about heredity all the time. Apparently you automatically take after your parents. That's why she says

I'm a degenerate, because I'm less good than she is. The idea of heredity terrifies me. I know that Mummy had a marvellous father she adored and a mother she hated. So which one is she like? Her father or her mother? As for me, I've no desire to be like anybody, but if I had to take after someone I'd rather it was Daddy.

For the moment, in spite of my heredity, Mummy tells me off for not being like her. I wonder whether as I grow up there's a danger of becoming more like her. There are some animals which change very suddenly when they become adult. I hope that if that happens to me, it won't be in a way which makes me like Mummy.

I'd rather be less good and have people hit me and not become like other people. Well, when I say other people ... For me, other people always means Mummy and Natalie. The rest come afterwards.

Would people have hit my soldier if he'd just taken me away with him, without asking permission? I expect so; and Mummy would have been the first. You have to be allowed to make other people happy. You have to have permission.

CHAPTER SEVEN

When I'm old enough to get married, if I fall in love with someone who doesn't want me I'll do the same as Daddy: I'll kill myself. Except I won't miss. It must be awful to try to kill yourself and to miss. You probably daren't start all over again and you're bound to be unhappy all your life.

Since I've been staying with her, Aunt Chloë has told me all about Daddy, and I feel very sad when I think about him. He can't love anybody now. That's why he's so peculiar.

Aunt Chloë made me swear not to mention it to anyone. Apparently Mummy insists we don't say anything, especially to Natalie who knows nothing about it. But Aunt Chloë is Daddy's sister.

Poor Daddy. I'd noticed, of course, that his right eye wasn't normal and that he had a scar on his temple, but I never guessed these were caused by shooting himself with a revolver when he was twenty years old for the sake of a lady who didn't want him.

They couldn't take the bullet out. It's still there, hidden behind his blue-white eye.

I wonder what happened to the lady, and whether she's happy. Since I heard about all this, I've felt tender towards Daddy. I think he was really unlucky to have met Mummy afterwards. He needed a wife who'd love him and comfort him. I'm only eleven, and there's nothing I can do to help him.

That's why, when you commit suicide for love, you absolutely mustn't miss. Otherwise life is so sad afterwards. I'd very much like to kiss Daddy one day. But I can't. He wouldn't understand, he'd push me away. Daddy isn't someone you can kiss. I don't even know if he and Mummy have ever kissed each other.

He really needs it, though. I can remember, when Thi Ba or Aunt Helene kissed me, it did me good. And the day that soldier kissed me, it left a mark deep down inside me which can never be wiped away. Even just thinking about it makes me want to cry. I hate crying, it makes me feel as if I can't defend myself any more. But sometimes my eyes start to cry, without my being able to do anything about it. Thank goodness, they only do it in private. Can Daddy's right eye still cry, or is it completely dead? When I heard the story about Daddy I was in the country, and that made it sadder still.

I loathe the country. To hear it described by other people, or in books, it sounds a very nice place, but living there is another matter. When it rains, which happens often and even right in the middle of August, you sink into the mud. When the weather is good it's invaded by flies and wasps. Besides, there are far too many animals in the country, especially at Aunt Chloë's, since she has a farm – which by the way she doesn't spend any time on, because she has a farmer to do that.

Cows, pigs and dogs I find terrifying. When I arrived, a few days ago, my aunt had a bitch called Katia, a hideous fat bulldog who slobbered and whose whole body was covered in fat folds of thick and yellowish skin.

In Hanoi, Thi Ba taught me to be very careful of dogs, and never to go near them. They might have rabies. Here apparently that doesn't happen, they're vaccinated. When I saw that enormous beast with her eyes popping out of her head and her fat swinging jowls, I was very frightened.

Aunt Chloë wasn't very pleased with me.

'Don't show her you're scared. When a dog sees you're afraid, it'll go for you.'

Of course, the more you're told not to show that you're scared the more scared you get. And sure enough, Katia hurled herself off the ground towards me, but the farmer caught her by the collar just in time. Her enormous open mouth was dribbling saliva right in front of my face.

They scolded her and shut her up in the kitchen. As for me, my heart was beating any old how and I couldn't breathe like you're meant to. But of course, it was my own fault. If I hadn't shown her I was afraid, nothing would have happened.

In my opinion, dogs have a wicked turn of mind. If people did the same, if every time that a person realised another person was scared he attacked them, it would be hell. But you can't tell that to people who keep dogs. I was shattered. The idea of having to spend a whole month near that dog appalled me. I was sure it'd turn out badly, that she'd end up killing me.

What saved me was that she attacked someone else. Someone she'd always known, who liked her, who wasn't scared of her: the farmer.

It happened in the courtyard of the farm. She started off just looking at the farmer. He was talking to my aunt, not paying any attention to the dog. After staring at him for a good while, she suddenly jumped and in a second, in a single bite, she tore half his face off. I saw it through the open window. It was horrible. That face transformed into a pile of flesh and crushed bone and blood, with one eye hanging out.

I threw up and for night after night I had screaming nightmares.

The farmer isn't dead. He's in the hospital, but he'll never be normal. Apparently even his brain was affected. My aunt said, 'Lucky I'm well insured.'

The farmer's wife and his two sons said nothing. An accident, it was an accident, wasn't it? No one can do anything about that. They're still working at the farm.

I've thought since, and the thought makes me very miserable, that if the farmer hadn't saved me the day before, this wouldn't have happened to him. It's like Hiroshima. I owe the fact that I'm still alive to Hiroshima, which caused thousands of deaths. Can you only survive if other people become victims? Like you can only eat by killing. And it's useless to become a vegetarian. Even plants get killed. It's less visible, that's all.

They killed Katia too. The vet came and gave her an injection. He said she'd gone mad. They don't look after mad animals, they kill them. I must admit that for me it was a great relief.

There are also a thousand chickens on this farm. They've all, or nearly all, got colds and it's my job to put drops in their noses twice a day. It's quite a business. For the ones which are dying and let themselves go, it does no good; they die anyway, in amorphous little heaps of feathers which seem so useless and unwanted, their eyes closed and their beaks turned away. The others fight it, and since they move around the whole time I can't remember which ones have been seen to and which haven't. Nothing looks more like a chicken than another chicken, especially when there are so many.

Aunt Chloë says being the chicken nurse gives me something to do. As if I needed her to find me something to do. Things are in general rather complicated with Aunt Chloë. She absolutely insists I should have lots of physical activity. I'm too much of a dreamer, too closed off, too steeped in my books. I ought to take up a sport, run, ride a bicycle or a horse. All those things are available in the country and I won't even take advantage of them! I refuse, I say they don't interest me. She doesn't understand, she gets upset.

'But surely you can't be as lazy as that!' She gets a bit angry, then she gives up.

'After all, I'm not your mother.'

And she starts talking about it again the next day. She won't give in, neither will I. I'm certainly not going to tell her that the doctor has forbidden me to do any of those things. I'm taking advantage of the fact that Mummy didn't think to tell her that my heart isn't very normal and I have problems with my breathing. For once, I'm with someone who doesn't know that I'm different and can't live exactly like other people, and I'm not going to waste the opportunity. Especially since Natalie, who is here on holiday with me, hasn't said anything. I think it's because she doesn't even remember I have this defect. She's never taken any notice of what happens to me.

I'd rather my aunt thought I was lazy. Most of the girls at my school are lazy. And they're normal, no one tells them they're different because of it.

However, I get on very well with Aunt Chloë. Perhaps because she's Daddy's sister, not Mummy's. And a curious phenomenon has happened. She and Natalie loathe each other. They hardly speak to each other, just the essential minimum. So Aunt Chloë takes a little bit of interest in me. It seems that physically I'm very like she was at my age. So she's bound to like me. Grown-ups adore it when you look like them. My handicap is that I don't look like enough people.

It surprises me that Aunt Chloë could have been like me. She has a completely round face with a double chin, and a swollen body which pushes out her clothes. When I follow her up the narrow stairs that lead from the dining room to her bedroom, I get the impression I'm behind a hot-air balloon. Beside me, who am all skin and bones, it makes a funny contrast. And another astonishing thing: Aunt Chloë listens to me talking. She's very attentive to everything I say. She finds my language surprising. I haven't dared tell her that I learned masses of words from the dictionary, on the quiet. I don't think it's forbidden, but I'm being careful. That dictionary isn't mine, so it's almost stealing.

Later on I'll arrange it so I have lots of things on my own and can take advantage of them all without using anything that belongs to someone else. I'm learning loads of things with Aunt Chloë. Some external, and others which concern me. I knew that Mummy was half Irish. She's very proud of it and often mentions it. On the subject of Mummy, my aunt pointed out to me that I never said Mummy, always 'she'. I hadn't realised. Now I'm more careful and I say Mummy. But I didn't know that Daddy wasn't completely French. It's like everything to do with him, it's secret, Mummy doesn't want it known. He has Norwegian blood and Mongolian blood. Norwegian's okay, but Mongolian is inferior blood, like yellow blood, according to Mummy: hence the secret.

Aunt Chloë, who looked me over very carefully, told me I had all the Mongol characteristics: almond eyes, high cheekbones, the palate inside my mouth convex instead of concave, and teeth all knitted to the bone of my jaw. What's more, I've got the mark of Genghis Khan in my hands.

Apparently Daddy is descended from Genghis Khan who was a fierce barbarian and a Mongol conqueror. This Genghis Khan had a certain blemish, and since he fathered loads of children here there and everywhere he only recognised the children which had the same defect as himself. They'd present him with babies, he'd examine their hands and say, 'This one is mine, that one isn't.'

Aunt Chloë has that defect, and so do I: it's the middle finger of each hand twisted slightly outwards, towards the little finger.

I looked at Natalie on the quiet, but she must be descended from someone other than Genghis Khan, because her fingers are absolutely straight. She has big brown eyes, whereas mine are very pale; hers aren't almond-shaped, and her cheekbones stick out much less than mine. Unfortunately I can't ask her to open her mouth so I can examine the inside.

Aunt Chloë has also helped me discover a marvellous aspect of life that I didn't know: the world of the cat. She has a little Siamese cat, only just three months old, who's called Angora and who has fur as soft as lukewarm velvet and eyes as blue as Daddy's good eye. Angora and I love each other.

All day long she follows me about, even when I go to look after the chickens, and when I have a bath she sits on the widest edge of the bath tub, behind my head. At night she comes to bed with me and stretches herself right along my body, squeezed tight against me. The first time it happened I didn't dare move. I ended up getting cramp. But now I know it doesn't matter if I move, she moves too and she doesn't abandon me.

I could put up with living in the country for ever, just for Angora's sake, even though it's not really my sort of place and it's so cold.

I'd have liked to introduce Angora to Thi Ba. And to my soldier. But I don't know if they like cats. Basically I don't know a thing about my soldier. As for Thi Ba, however

hard I try I can't think of anything to do with liking cats —
even though I'm sure I remember everything she ever said
to me.

It's weird: I forget what I'm taught at school all the time
and I get lots of bad marks because of it. That school
isn't interested in me, so I've no wish to listen. But I can
remember perfectly everything Thi Ba told me to help me
to understand life. It's written in my head like in a book.
With Thi Ba I understood everything; here it's hard because
the words are all made for white people.

Even so, I came top of the class once, by accident, a long
time ago at the end of my first year at school. At that time
I was still little and still thought I ought to try very hard,
so I worked in secret, in my bed at night.

I occasionally got good marks, purely by chance, and
then one week there was a sort of miracle: I was top of the
class. At school everyone else was as astonished as I was.

They gave me the little metal cross they put on your
blouse to show that you're top, and take off when you
aren't any longer. My hands trembled so much I only just
managed to pin it on.

It didn't seem very fair to me, but I didn't care. On the
way home from school I felt like shouting my happiness to
everyone I saw. I thought Mummy would be pleased and
proud of me, and that she'd see I might get to know as
many things as Natalie if I took a lot of trouble.

When I got home I was all excited and the maid asked
me if I had a temperature. I told her all about it and she
burst out laughing.

'There's no reason to get yourself into such a state,' she
said, a bit scoldingly, but she was laughing so much as she
told me off that she couldn't stop herself and her eyes were
crying.

I put my things away and then went to look at myself in the mirror in the bathroom, to see what I looked like with that little cross the head nun had pinned onto my blouse. But I was just the same, and my hair was a mess and I was redder than usual. I combed my hair, in honour of my cross, wetting the comb so that my hair went all over the place a bit less, and then I decided not to say anything, for it to be a surprise, to wait till Mummy discovered my cross for herself.

But she didn't notice it.

After dinner I couldn't hold back any longer and I announced my great news.

She looked at me without smiling, with the expression she has when she's bored, and she said, 'Good.'

Just as she'd have said 'Good' if I'd told her the sun was shining. I'm on the lookout for the sun all the time, but she doesn't like it. She maintains that it squashes all the colours, kills them. And that what's more it's uncomfortable.

I went off to bed, as usual, without anyone saying anything else to me. Nothing had changed, I was the same, top of the class or not. I cried a little, not really, only enough to wet a small handkerchief.

But I felt so sad for my poor cross, which would have been so much better on another little girl, since no one here was interested in it, that I pinned it on to my nightie so as not to abandon it on my blouse, and we slept together.

In the morning, when I got up, I saw Mummy looking at me oddly, but she didn't say anything.

It was that evening, when I got back from school, that I found out what she was thinking. She was in the sitting room, having tea with a friend from Paris. She was talking about me, making fun of me.

'Poor Laurence is a cretin,' she was saying (and she was

laughing, she never laughs in front of me), 'she never has a normal reaction to things. For once she came top of her class, and anyone would think it was a huge event! Suddenly she thinks she's a child genius, she even pinned her cross to her nightie!'

'Oh, you know,' answered the lady from Paris, a lady I don't like whose mouth turns down towards the ground, 'you know, Charlotte, children are often absolutely ridiculous!'

Perhaps that lady was never a child herself?

I took off my cross and put it in my pocket. Not for long. The next week I wasn't top any more and I gave it back. Since then it's all the same to me whether or not I understand what they're saying in class. I don't try any more.

It's all the same to me, too, when Mummy yells at me for getting bad marks. All I have to do is lift my right arm to protect my face when she gets really annoyed.

Now, when the nuns explain things that don't interest me, I turn inwards, into myself, inside my heart. I think about Thi Ba and her gentle way of talking, so different to the people here with their hard voices.

In Hanoi, in the street, the people often shouted at each other when they spoke, but never Thi Ba.

'I can't stand soft women,' Mummy says.

To listen to Thi Ba, I used to put myself close to her, my body against hers, close enough to smell her smell of nuoc-mâm, betel, and the oil she put on her hair to soften it.

She hardly ever used to touch me. Only once or twice did she ever kiss me in the white way. When she wanted to show me I was important to her, she would breathe in across my face. In the Indochinese way. She used to say it gave you the pleasure of a kiss without the sweat and the disgusting saliva. Even when you shut your mouth, the saliva is still there inside. And anyhow in Hanoi it's too hot to kiss with your mouth.

What would it be like if Mummy kissed me one day? Perhaps I'd hate it? Anyhow, Mummy wouldn't know how to breathe across my face. But I wonder whether she knows how to kiss, even the white way. I've never seen her kiss anyone, not even Natalie.

In any case, Natalie hates to be touched. She can't even bear anyone to take her hand. She says it makes her want to vomit. Personally I loathe it when people I don't like put their hands on me, but when it's someone who lives in my heart I only want one thing: to roll myself into a ball and snuggle into their body, or as close as possible.

Since Aunt Helene, no one has kissed me. In any way. I don't know which I miss the most: for someone to sniff my face or someone to put their mouth against me.

The marvellous thing about cats is that you can cuddle up to them and kiss them as much as you want. It feels all soft in your mouth, and they love it and they show it: they purr. I'm sure that if you have nobody to love, you could always find a cat to live in your arms. Maybe later on I could have a cat? Even if I've got my soldier?

As for my soldier, since the Gare de l'Est I don't believe in him much any more. It's been too long and I'm sure I no longer exist in his mind. If I manage to find him later on, will he accept me anyway? Perhaps he's picked up another little girl in the meantime? If he's got another little girl I won't stand a chance because she'll obviously be better than me.

Later on . . . I feel a bit frightened about what my later on is going to be like. With being different and being useless at school, what can I hope for? Not much, I don't think.

I still don't know what I want to do when I no longer depend on Mummy. Get married, perhaps, but I don't know whether that'd suit me. I couldn't stand to live like Mummy and Daddy. I'd like to get married in another way. To someone like that Strasbourg soldier who'd take me in his arms and give me masses of tenderness. But maybe it's not so easy for someone who's different to get themselves loved.

What I like most about Aunt Chloë is that she's always led a very interesting life. A life that horrifies Mummy. She sometimes talks to Daddy about it in a hard, nasty voice.

'Your sister – she's a disgrace to the family!'

Aunt Chloë ran away from home when she was seventeen. She was in love with a boy who wasn't from the same social class and her parents wouldn't even have him in the house. One evening, she ran off to live with him at the other end of France and she never wanted to go back.

After many years, she realised she wasn't happy any more. She fell in love with another man and ran away again. And she's done that all her life. She's never worked, she's always been 'kept'.

At the moment she's with a middle-aged man. He's married, he's got four children, and he lives about thirty miles away. It was him who bought her this farm. Every other day he comes to lunch or to dinner. Afterwards he stays for quite a while in her bedroom and then he goes away again.

I really like this gentleman. He's nice, he smiles easily and he smells good.

Even if it's not done I'd much prefer to live like Aunt Chloë than like Mummy. Actually, Aunt Chloë is someone who's different too. And in her different way she tried to teach me about things.

'When you're older and you go out with boys, choose carefully. That's the important thing: don't go with just anybody. The first criterion is to find a generous one. A man who isn't generous is narrow, selfish, incapable of love and incapable of making a woman happy. The important thing is not that he should be rich. If he is, all the better, life is so much more pleasant when you've got money! But have a poor generous one rather than a mean rich one. A man ought to give you presents. He should find out what you like, what'd please you, and do everything he can to get it. You see, it's the time he spends looking for the presents that proves how much you mean to him. Tell yourself that a bunch of flowers very carefully chosen and given to you by a poor man who's made an effort can be much more important than a piece of jewellery given by someone rich, but chosen by his secretary. If the man is generous and he loves you, he should be ready to give you everything. I really mean everything. A man in love will skin himself for the women in his life. I've ruined men. I'm sure that they loved me, those ones. As for the others . . . Second thing: a man who loves you never leaves you alone. He has only one thought in his head: to live with you, to be parted from you as seldom as possible, even if he has to sacrifice lots of things to do it. I don't believe in great discussions about love, I believe in proof. And those two things – spending all he's got, and living for you, with you – are the only things that matter. You understand?'

Yes I understand. I understand that much better than all the things Mummy and the nuns say. But unfortunately what I can't see so clearly is who would ever want to ruin himself for me.

Aunt Chloë gave a great sigh.

'You know, Laurence, I used to be pretty and I'm not

any more. So now I've settled down with a man who loves me, but not enough to leave everything and come and live with me. I make myself content with it, I've no longer got any choice. What comforts me is that I have really been loved, and I've really loved in return. It's the only thing in life that counts, love. It's more important than anything, even if it can hurt very badly. A woman who hasn't lived through at least one great love has skirted round the edge of her life.'

Am I going to skirt round the edge of my life?

CHAPTER EIGHT

I've lost an eye. But it's worth it because I've got a friend.

At least, I hope it's worth it. My eye is spoiled for my whole life but I can't be sure that Marie-Claire won't abandon me one day.

I've had too much experience to live in a dream.

It wouldn't be fair if my left eye had been killed for ever but I'd only been given Marie-Claire for a few months. But who could I tell that it wasn't fair?

In any case I'm glad for my eye: it has been well fixed up and now nobody can see what happened to it. It looks the same as the other one, it moves normally and I'm not completely one-eyed. If I close my right eye I can still see whether it's dark or light and I can make out blurry coloured shapes.

Of course, my crippled eye will never be any use to me, but if I say nothing, it'll be like my heart, nobody will notice. That's the important thing. I got out of it pretty well.

Basically, I'm very lucky. I should have been dead a long time ago, I should have an eye like Daddy's, but here I am alive and well and when I look at myself in the mirror I see nothing abnormal.

Losing my left eye was my own fault, as usual. Why did I have to meddle in something that was none of my business? I'm supposed to be apart from the rest, my new nickname is 'the savage', I know how to stay in my little corner and not get in anyone's way. The first rule when you don't want to bother people is never to say what you think . . . What came over me?

In class we have to sit at desks two by two in alphabetical order. To add to my misery I was put beside a little pest whose idea of fun is doing nasty things to other people. She steals all the time. Which doesn't bother me. But she manages to get other people blamed for it. For no reason; she doesn't even need to save her own skin. Her latest little joke is to steal something from one girl and then hide it in another girl's pocket. Whom she then tells on ... Obviously, the poor girl can't stick up for herself. Grown-ups never take the trouble to go into things properly or to understand anything.

No one understands even now. But I caught her at her little game and like an idiot, a month ago, I started telling her what I thought of her, in a low voice so the teacher couldn't hear. She didn't say a word. She picked up her compasses from the black desk and, while I was looking her straight in the face as I talked, to show her how angry I was, she shoved the point of the compasses into my left eye.

It hurt, but I didn't understand what had happened to me straight away. It was Ursula, the little pest, who realised before I did. She started screaming and crying, and writhed about in her seat as if the whole class had fallen on top of her. Of course, they all came rushing over.

I didn't move; I couldn't have made a sound. I was trying not to cry, to forget how much it hurt. It was Marie-Claire who turned everyone's attention on to me. She shouted, 'Hey, have you seen what she's done? Look at Laurence's eye!'

I don't know what my eye was like, but it must have been peculiar because there was a general panic.

The geometry teacher sent someone to fetch the head, who rang up Mummy; she arrived straight away and we went off, me and her, to the doctor. Mummy was very angry and told me off.

'What on earth did you do to make her attack you like that? You are such a difficult child, it's unbelievable. If only I'd known . . .'

I hardly bothered to listen. I was having trouble finding a new way of walking. With just one eye nothing seemed the same any more. I was protecting the eye that had been attacked as carefully as I could, holding my dirty handkerchief to it with my left hand.

Life gets singularly complicated by having only one eye. In a month I've had time to realise. I've become terribly clumsy. Everything is difficult. Stairs especially, and the distance between things. I have to think about every movement. When I pour out a cup of tea, for example, I tend to pour it to one side of the cup. So of course I get told off all the time.

'Can't you be a bit more careful!'

If my eye looks as good as new it's thanks to the doctor, who has been marvellous. He put some liquid into it, and covered it up with a nice thick white compress held on by sticky plaster, then he said to Mummy:

'Bring her back to see me every day, as soon as she gets out of school, for two weeks.'

Mummy said yes but she forgot. Naturally she has other things on her mind. Natalie had just had her eighteenth birthday and made her debut into the world. She can officially look for a husband at last. But it costs a fortune, the whole business. The dressmaker has made her eight long dresses for going to parties, and two cloaks as well. She's also got to have handbags, shoes, gloves. Natalie is very difficult, she wants the best of everything. I don't find all this much fun because now they can't buy me anything any more, and since I've grown a lot since last year I can no longer get into my coat and my two pairs of shoes both hurt my feet horribly. The hems of my skirts have been let down, and it doesn't matter much if my sweaters stop before they get to the ends of my arms and my waist, but it's amazing how cold this country can be in winter without a coat. I've got a jacket, a tight one, which I can still manage to squeeze into; it's the one I wore last summer, but it's made of thick cotton and I shiver the whole time. I've always got a cold and I cough a lot, which irritates Mummy.

'Stop coughing, it gets on my nerves!'

And then she adds, with what she calls her 'black sense of humour', 'Die if you must, but do it quietly!'

Anyway, Mummy is so taken up with the work involved in finding a husband for Natalie that the next day she had forgotten she had to take me to the doctor. When I got home from school she was out shopping with Natalie. I took the opportunity to go into the kitchen to chat to Charlotte, the maid. She's the only person in the house I have real conversations with, but I can only have them on the quiet because it's a thing that's not done. I was in the middle of asking her if she thought I'd have an eye like Daddy's, or if it'd fix itself, when the telephone rang. I went to answer it. It was the doctor. He wanted to speak to Mummy. I explained where she was. There was a silence at first, then he said, 'Come over here straight away.'

I couldn't, of course, I didn't have any money to pay him, doctors are too expensive, those are not the sort of amounts you can steal, and in any case I couldn't remember where he was. So I said no, very politely, it wasn't possible, but he's so extraordinary, that gentleman, he can guess what's going on in your mind, and he spoke to me very nicely.

'Listen, you're going to come and see me every day, straight from school. I'll explain where I live. You go to the Place du Trocadéro, you know it, it's close to where you live, then you take the Avenue d'Eylau.' Then he added, 'You don't need any money, you don't have to pay anything. All right? So come right away. If you don't you'll end up with a very ugly eye. I can't give you back your sight, but I can preserve the appearance of your eye. And appearances are important, don't you think? You're a very pretty little girl, do you want to have an empty white eye which will spoil your looks?'

I said no, of course not, and I went.

After that, the doctor explained to me that I shouldn't hold it against Mummy if she was rather peculiar. But why should I hold it against her? She doesn't look for ways to hurt me, I'm a burden to her, that's different. And anyway she doesn't realise. To realise what's happening to other people you have to think about them, and she never has time to think about me. Or if she does, it's because she's forced to, and that's a nuisance for her.

As far as she's concerned, what happened to me is just a little bump, a bit of a scratch. She doesn't even know I can't see out of that eye now. And *I'm* certainly not going to tell her! I've given her enough problems of that sort. But personally, if pushed, I must admit what would suit me best would be for her to forget that I exist altogether. Unfortunately, that can't happen as long as I'm dependent on her.

I often think about the fact that when I was born, everything went wrong. They had to take out the whole of the inside of her belly. She will never be able to forgive me for that. It's twelve years now since it happened. An eternity. But I'm sure she hasn't forgotten. Every time she stares at me her face closes in around her eyes, and I think she's remembering it. It must be a terrible operation when they take out the whole of the inside of your belly. Much worse than being one eye short.

Following this 'deplorable accident', as the head of the school calls it (I mean my eye, not Mummy's belly), they separated Ursula and me. She was put in Marie-Claire's place and Marie-Claire now sits next to me. Because of me, it has been pointed out, the alphabetical order has been disrupted. I'm very pleased to be beside Marie-Claire, but the fact that Ursula is just behind me fills me with panic. I'm always wondering if she's going to attack me from the back, and I daren't turn round. I don't want to let her see I'm frightened.

Naturally, Ursula never says a word to me. Whis is no loss. In class everyone is embarrassed, and since it happened no one has dared ask me about my eye. Not even the nuns.

This sort of event should never occur in a religious institution for young girls from good families, so they pretend it just didn't take place. It's one solution, when things seem too much of a nuisance. With me, Daddy has always behaved like this. Last week, when I got on to the bus which runs from school to the house and which means I can get there more quickly and comfortably than on foot, when I manage to get hold of a ticket, I sat down beside Daddy, who was already on it.

He saw that someone in a skirt had sat down next to him, so he took off his hat, something he always does in front of ladies, and then put it back on his head.

If he'd recognised me he would never have done that. So I explained to him:

'It's me, Daddy. Laurence.'

He was very surprised. He turned to me and said, 'What are you doing on this bus?'

I told him, but I don't know if he heard. In any case, he didn't say anything more. I felt embarrassed, ill at ease. I should never have sat down beside him. Luckily there are only three stops and the journey passed quite quickly.

Marie-Claire lives two streets away from me, which is extremely convenient when you want to see each other as much as she and I do. I daren't take her to my house, and I loathe hanging around the streets when it's so cold and I haven't any extra clothes for protection. But she can take me to her house as often as she likes, it doesn't cause the slightest problem and her mother even seems pleased to see me. Every day when we get out of school, I go home with Marie-Claire and her mother makes us afternoon tea with as much butter and jam as we want, and hot chocolate. It's absolutely delicious and I'm never hungry now.

All in all I'm much happier since I've had one eye missing. I don't feel lonely any more. I only hope that if I find Thi Ba and my soldier again, they won't notice I've got this spoilt eye. I must learn to be less clumsy, so they won't realise anything is wrong.

I'm a bit frightened all the same, because in the mirror I see myself as normal, but I don't know if my right eye is good enough to let me see what I really look like. I wonder if people with two eyes in good condition see me differently and if they think my eye has become as ugly as Daddy's. I'm also afraid it might only be fixed for the time being and one day it might end up going wrong. I'd have liked to ask the doctor all these questions, but I didn't dare. He'd already been so kind about looking after me without being paid that I didn't want to burden him more with all my questions.

I owe him a lot, that doctor, and I'm very annoyed that I don't really know how to show it. I'd be glad to go and see him from time to time, but I couldn't, he has masses of sick people waiting to see him and no time to spare. And I couldn't steal some money to give him a present, either; it would seem like wanting to pay him for what he'd done for me. I could have prayed to my modelling clay buddha, but he's dead. Charlotte, the maid, swept underneath my bed one day, something she'd never done before, incidentally, and she threw him out with the dust. All the same it was a dreadful death for a buddha, even one made of modelling clay. And it was my own fault again, I ought to have found him a better hiding place. Until my skewered eye and the entry of Marie-Claire into my heart, I missed my modelling-clay buddha horribly. He was my only friend, and I had no one else to talk to. Now I chat to Marie-Claire, but I still have one problem: not letting her see that I'm different. So I talk about everything except myself, and it's very complicated because it's mostly about yourself that you want to talk. With my buddha it was easier, I could tell him everything. The great advantage of buddhas is that you never need to lie to them. White people always get angry when they find out you're lying, as if you lied for fun. Telling lies is hard, it's not enjoyable, and you do it because you can't get by any other way. I'm well aware that Natalie lies less than me, but it's because she has less need to, that's all. I'd very much like to do as she does, but generally I don't have the choice.

When I was little, Thi Ba lied for me. She lied to the yellow people to make them forget I was white, and she lied to the whites because there's nothing else you can do with whites. I got into the habit of telling lies all by myself. Even with Marie-Claire, in the end I have to do what I do

137

with other white people: I can't tell her everything. Apart from Thi Ba and my soldier, I've never really been able to talk. I've nobody to help me and tell me what I should do. In my way, I mean. The nuns spend their entire time telling you what you should and shouldn't do, but it's always things which go against my grain, or things which are stupid. This morning, again, there was one of them who explained that you must never look at a man below the belt. As if it could be bad to look at a gentleman's trousers! Whites really have a funny idea of education.

If Thi Ba was still with me, I'd know how to behave. How to show my gratitude to that doctor, for instance. There's nothing more complicated than gratitude. How can you tell when you should be grateful, and when you shouldn't? Thi Ba taught me to be careful about that. She used to say that people expect you to be grateful when they've done nothing special for you, or only the things they had to do. Mummy, for example: she says I'm an ungrateful creature and that I ought to be thankful for all she does for me. But she hasn't really got any choice. That's the problem. Gratitude should be reserved for those who could have done otherwise than help you.

It can also happen that you help someone by accident, without wanting to. But in a case like that you can't ask for thanks, or expect presents. The only thing to do is be glad you were able to bring a bit of pleasure without causing yourself any trouble. Perhaps that's Nirvana: making everyone happy without giving yourself any pain.

There is no gratitude in Nirvana, I'm sure. There, behaving well to other people must be a completely natural thing, and it must happen to everybody. Here on earth, gratitude is important, because it's rare for anyone to do something good for nothing. That's why, if someone gives you a little bit of happiness, they generally want you to pay for it.

I've made a list of the people to whom I owe a debt of gratitude. There's Thi Ba, first of all, and then my soldier, Aunt Helene, Aunt Chloë and now the eye doctor. I feel a bit ashamed: I haven't put Mummy on the list.

CHAPTER NINE

The child of the red land. I'm going to kill the child of the red land.

No one will ever be able to shut us up together again, that child and me. We'll be free. You're only free when you no longer exist. There is nothing at all after death, I'm sure of that now. Nobody to make you suffer. Emptiness. Instead of love, sadness, hurt. Too many words jostle each other in my head. When I've killed myself there will be no more words. From one moment to the next I shall be nothing more than a pile of flesh and bones which will disappear, little by little.

Poor little child of the red land. It's a bore having to kill her, but I've no choice. I can't kill myself and let her stay alive. I love her though, this child who is myself, invented by me. She has my name and my character. But she's better than me, of course, and she's had a different life, a much better one, which I invented for her. Her nickname, 'child of the red land', isn't one that I chose; it was Jacques. When I told him the story of my fake childhood, the one I made up for him, he stroked my hair, very gently, just like my soldier in Hanoi, and he said, 'For me, you'll always be the child of the red land.'

So. That was the day she came into being; I had changed my past.

The red land is a beautiful place, a superb place, there's nowhere more wonderful. Thi Ba, who'd travelled a lot, had told me about it and I found out about it again in a book of Aunt Chloë's.

It's a vast stretch of earth the colour of blood, in the

south of my country, close to Saigon, and on that land there is nothing but rubber plantations. No villages, no towns, just trees and the houses of the planters.

That's where I was born and where I lived until I came to France. Mummy gave birth to me without any trouble, and I had nothing to be guilty about. She wanted a little girl and she was delighted when I arrived. She took on Thi Ba to help her, and so I had two mothers.

I've also got a grandmother, like the children here, but a much better one than any of theirs. A bâ-gia who's not really old, just a bit aged on the outside, but not in her heart, pretty, sweet and tender, who laughs all the time, with glints of gold in her blue eyes. Her name is Aurora and she's a real Mongol, but she doesn't hide it; on the contrary, she's proud of it and she shows everyone her hands, which are the same as mine.

My grandmother was lucky: she stayed out there, at our home. She's very happy and she has lots of delicious things to eat.

She lives in our big house, which is very beautiful, with its lacquered ceilings as shiny as mirrors, its red Chinese furniture and other furniture in green or white rattan, marble on the floors and an immense terrace lined with flowers. My bedroom is mauve, with a big low bed where I sleep with Thi Ba.

I drew a plan of the house and I showed it to Jacques. He said he'd never seen such a lovely house, and I thought to myself that I'd struggle all my life but one day I'd have a real house like that. How much money would you need for a house like that? A fortune, I suppose. It must represent piles of coats and an enormous quantity of food.

But after all I could easily relearn how to eat hardly anything, and do without a coat like I did last year.

True, I'm forgetting that I'm going to kill myself and that I won't have that sort of problem ever again. Or any other sort.

There are moments when I forget I have no future.

It's extraordinary to be able to condemn yourself to death. In the end it's the only freedom one has. Nobody can force you not to die.

It's a month since I made the decision. At least — not exactly. It was only if . . .

A month ago, when she locked me in my room without telling me how long it was for, I decided that if I was still locked up when my birthday came, and if she didn't take me to see *The White Horse Inn* as she promised, there would be nothing left for me but to kill myself. Besides, life without Jacques doesn't appeal to me. I love him too much, I'm too unhappy without him. You can't live apart from someone you love. I can't, in any case. I have a clumsy heart which knocks itself against everything it comes across.

I'm thirteen years old today and I feel terribly grown up, even though the doctor who certified I was a virgin said that I was childish and young for my age. Maybe I haven't got a thirteen-year-old body, but in my mind I'm much older than that. Children don't think about killing themselves. They have only one thought: to survive. I remember very clearly the child I really was, not my invented self. When Thi Ba left, I suffered just as much, but I didn't want to die.

I don't know when I became an adult. Whether it happened all at once, or by little bits, but that's how it is. Dying is no joke, even if it's your own decision, but it's so good to be able to tell yourself you won't ever suffer any more. There's another advantage too: your defects no longer matter. My heart, my hands which are too small, my retarded body, none of that has any importance now. When I die, all my defects will die themselves. So why do they matter so much, these failings, when you're alive? Does it take dying for them to become unimportant?

What has always astonished me is that people daren't speak ill of the dead. Isn't it done? Why not? Dead people couldn't care less if you speak ill of them, but living people can be very badly hurt by it. I suppose it's a kind of superstition, a fear that the dead might take revenge. In some countries, men offer food to the dead, but not to the living. Yet it's the living who are hungry, not the dead. I don't believe it's done out of goodness, it's simply calculation. The people aren't giving, they're protecting themselves.

I'd very much have liked to have been protected myself. Not necessarily all the time – you can't ask for too much, and you mustn't live in a dream – but from time to time. To have someone strong who loved me and whose arms were a refuge.

Actually, I was lucky, even if I didn't realise it. I had Thi Ba for five years, before she went away.

Thi Ba used to say to me, 'The day you get your periods, you'll be grown up and you won't need anyone any more.' I feel very grown up, but still incapable of not needing anyone. And I haven't even got my periods yet. How retarded am I? I don't know. I can't talk to the doctor, I see him with Mummy. She says whatever she wants and I just get examined like an animal.

Besides, I never go to the doctor. Except when they wanted to look inside my belly, because of Jacques. Because of my heart, perhaps? Is the doctor allowed to forbid me to go to school if he noticed that my heart is all askew?

They've forbidden me to do sports and gymnastics, anyway.

Also forbidden is kissing a boy. Even Jacques. But I wanted to so much.

About Jacques: I loved him straight away. When Marie-Claire said to me, that Thursday afternoon, 'This is my cousin,' I looked at him and I wished for only one thing: to sit down at his feet and put my head on his knees.

I don't know whether or not he's handsome. I don't think so. But he is himself, that's more handsome than anything. When I saw him, so tall, with his beige velvet trousers which were too short and his crepe soles which stuck to the floor with a funny noise, his green eyes like my soldier's and his over-long hands, I belonged to him immediately.

I told myself buddha had to help me, to make him love me.

Buddha did help me. Jacques didn't see that I was an outsider, different, a failed yellow person disguised as a white. He didn't reject me. He asked me lots of questions. So I told him all about a made-up me, who was myself all the same in my mind, and he fell in love. For real. It was so incredible that it could only have come from buddha.

He wrote to me. No one had ever written to me before. Nobody. And of course I answered. How can you love someone without wanting to write to them? I would have written to him day and night if I'd dared.

He gave me a radio, a real one, like other people have, one which works. I put it in my bed and hug it in my arms when I go to sleep, to feel that I'm with him. He also gave me a dagger which opens letters and which comes from Toledo, in Spain. Every year, Jacques goes to Spain on holiday. His parents have a house in that country, by the sea. Jacques adores Spain, he wants to take me there later on. It seems so beautiful, Spain. Perhaps it's as good as

Indochina? I wonder if you can go barefoot and sit on the ground in Spain?

Jacques and I saw each other every Thursday for nine weeks. That meant I had six days to wait, each week. He and Marie-Claire went roller-skating at the Trocadéro, and I watched. I learned to take part in my mind. Anyway, even if I'd been normal, since the business with the priest I don't steal any more and so I can't have any more things. Roller-skates must be very expensive.

I watched them and felt as if I was with them. I loved them both, in different ways. Marie-Claire was so pretty, with her breasts and her hair floating in time with her movements. And as for him, he skated seriously, like a professor, and from time to time his eyes would lift to look at me.

I used to wonder when they'd have had enough, because I wanted them with me for longer, and what time it was on their watches, but I never dared say anything and I waited without moving, admiring them and dreaming in my heart. I dreamed for myself a whole life with those two, a life of tenderness, a happy life in my red land.

When they came back to me they'd be out of breath, happy, and I'd tell myself I was so lucky to be with them. But we'd have very little time left. It takes a long time, roller-skating. Jacques would tell me he loved me, Marie-Claire would laugh, and we'd have to go home.

And wait another six days. It's unbelievable how long that can seem, six days.

When I love someone it's in a different way, it's absolute, it's not like other people. It would never enter my head to go and do something that pleased me when I only had a few hours to spend with the person I loved. I'd rather talk to him, look at him, touch him. Nothing could count for as much. But obviously I'm less fun than roller-skating. So if I kill myself what would it matter, since even roller-skating is more interesting than me?

The ninth week was the great scene. I didn't feel that I was loved as much as I loved, but it was more than I hoped for all the same, and it could have gone on if it hadn't been for that nun. Like an idiot I hadn't seen her, the nun, even though she's from my school, and it must be said that those nuns disguise themselves in ordinary clothes to trick the world into thinking they're normal women. We're obliged to wear uniform, but they're not. She was there in front of us, watching us, but I didn't see her because I wasn't interested in anyone apart from Jacques and Marie-Claire. Jacques had sat down beside me, because the laces on his skates had come undone, and I was so happy to feel him against me that I kissed him, suddenly, very hard, hugging him to me. He laughed and he kissed me too, just as hard, and we both had red cheeks.

The nun didn't say anything to us, she just went back to school and summoned Mummy.

'Your daughter kisses boys in public. It's disgraceful, scandalous! She is expelled from the school!'

At home Mummy screamed; she never screams when she's out.

'You're a little whore! You've slept with him – admit it!'

I said I didn't know what she was talking about. It was poor Thi Ba's fault, again. Mummy started going on about her.

'No one should ever give a child an Annamese nurse. They stroke the babies to send them to sleep and they grow up to be perverted children.'

I don't know whether Thi Ba stroked me when I was a baby, but I hope she did. I loved to be stroked. I remember

146

when my soldier caressed my hair, just for a second, or when Aunt Helene rocked me in her arms, it was so good.

Mummy got an appointment with the doctor and they put me on a table and pushed my legs apart to look at the inside of me.

By a piece of luck I was still a virgin, otherwise they would have put me in prison.

Oddly enough, Daddy put in an appearance at this point. He took his belt and he beat me with it, very hard. I was rolling on the floor, crying. I was trying above all to protect my good eye with my hands. It hurts, being hit in the eyes with a belt.

I haven't seen Jacques again. I'll never see him again. They've locked me up ever since I came back from the doctor. I'm let out to go to the bathroom. Not for long. They bring me meals on a tray. It's July 18th, and I'm thirteen today. I won't go on holiday, I don't care.

But Jacques. I can't, I won't live without Jacques. We could have got married later on, Jacques and I, if not for those terrible nuns. He's three years older than me, which was good. Thi Ba used to say that if a woman marries a man older than herself, the age difference must be an uneven number. Otherwise the marriage won't be happy.

Jacques has telephoned several times. I heard, because the telephone is in the dining room, next to my bedroom. Mummy was very amiable; she used the polite voice she puts on with strangers.

'I'm so sorry, but Laurence doesn't want to talk to you. There's no point in phoning again.'

So there we are. That's the end of Jacques. And of me too.

I go into the bathroom that's part of my room, just separated off by a curtain. I look at myself in the mirror, and to test myself out I wonder what I'll look like when I'm dead.

Jacques. I haven't got the right words, the gestures other people use, I don't know anything other people know, but I love you so much.

What use would it be to me to go on living without Jacques? Life without him is a horror.

The fact is, I'm clumsy all round. I don't even know how to kill myself. I've been thinking about it for a month now but I still haven't found the best way. I live on the fourth floor. It'd be easy. But I'm scared of heights and like an idiot I always draw back. A real retard, as Mummy says.

Strangle myself with a belt? I've tried it out, but it's very complicated. There's always a moment when you let go. Hang myself? Where, and with what? Swallowing something would be best. I suppose that emptying the whole medicine cupboard could see to it.

They've locked me up, which doesn't makes things any easier. Locked up as a punishment, and also so that I don't go to Jacques. I admit that if I could, I'd try to see him again straight away. The law, and everything they could do to me, what does any of that matter? Thi Ba ran off, my soldier was taken away from me and now they've deprived me of Jacques.

There's nothing left but dying.

I know I'll find a way. I've never had a watch, I don't know what time it is, but Mummy has already gone off to Châtelet with Natalie, so it must be quite late. Daddy is here, but he's shut himself away in his study, as usual. My only means of access to the medicine cupboard is Antoinette, the new maid. Mummy is very pleased to have a new maid, because the one before was called Charlotte, the same as her, and of course she was obliged to call her

Marie and the maid refused to reply to that name since it wasn't her own and that created all sorts of problems which don't occur now. Antoinette is very kind to me. From time to time she brings me books or sweets in secret. In the evenings, when Mummy goes out with Natalie, she comes to see me. It's easy: Mummy leaves the key in the door, on the outside. Sometimes, when she can, Antoinette comes in the daytime too. I like it very much but the problem is that she asks me questions about my childhood all the time, but I can't tell her anything. So she thinks I'm sulking, or being, as she calls it, a crosspatch. The bore is that I can't tell her the story of the red land. It's very difficult to be around people who know your family. Having a double childhood gets very complicated in the end.

But the advantage of imagination is that it allows you to live all the things you want in your head. Without my imagination, I think I'd have liked my life even less. Through the six days of each week I waited to see Jacques, I used to pretend we were still together ... We went for walks hand in hand, occasionally he stroked my hair, and I had some money to buy him presents with. Mummy would have called that sort of imagining 'shopgirl daydreams', but it helped me.

Basically, I'm not very brave. I look for help all the time. But in a few hours' time I'll no longer have any need of anyone. Not even Jacques. The red land won't exist.

Love stories usually have an unhappy ending, in books and in real life. Sometimes, with a bit of luck, they turn out all right, and sometimes they can transform people too.

It's ten o'clock. Antoinette, who let me out of my room for a while because it's my birthday, has locked me up again so she doesn't get into trouble with Mummy. She's gone off to bed. I kissed her and she was astonished. I'm not absolutely crazy about Antoinette but I wanted so much to kiss someone before I died. Usually the condemned person asks for a cigarette. What I need is a bit of tenderness.

I walked around the apartment for an hour. In complete freedom. All I had to do was avoid Daddy's room. He's already gone to bed and he's reading. He coughs a little from time to time. He must have got a chill.

For a long while I gazed around the apartment, for the last time. I finally decided I don't like it. I find it depressing. Mummy claims that it's extremely beautiful and that the furniture is superb, priceless. To me, all those walls and beige curtains, those glassy pictures which seem to have been painted by artists without dreams, that dark enormous furniture, just seem sad.

Even so, I stroked the furniture as I went past, to say goodbye.

I wonder where Mummy would have shut me up if her friends had still been here and I'd still been sleeping in the hall. Perhaps in the boxroom, with the suitcases, like when I was little and she thought I'd been naughty. But there's no window there, no room for a bed . . .

I rummaged in the medicine cupboard without finding anything of interest. In fact it's not so easy to kill yourself.

Eventually it was Antoinette who gave me the solution, without suspecting it. Apparently some mice have been playing about in the kitchen for the last few days, and she was looking everywhere for the packet of rat poison Mummy bought today. Mummy is so untidy that it could have been anywhere. It was me who found it, but I didn't say anything; I went and hid it in my bedroom. Then I wrote a note to Mummy, because I thought it would be more polite to say goodbye to her before I died, and I put it on her pillow:

Dear Mummy,

I'll never be like I should. I'm not Natalie, I'm not pretty enough or clever enough, and most of all my heart is too clumsy. So I'd rather kill myself, because it'll be easier for me and for everyone else. Especially for you, since you'll at last be rid of all the problems I cause. I'm terribly sorry about the rat poison, but you'll have to buy some more. I hope it's not too expensive. There's no need to bury me in a box. You can just burn me and throw me away, it's better and I'm sure it's cheaper. A burial must cost at least as much as a dress for Natalie.

Good night.

Laurence.

P.S. *Was The White Horse Inn good?*

There. That's all I put. I hope it's enough, and I hope I didn't make any spelling mistakes. It's amazing how hard it is to swallow rat poison. It's like flour with a horrible taste. I've eaten the whole packet, just to be on the safe side, because they put the doses to use for rats, and not for people, and you must need much bigger quantities. With each mouthful I drank some water to wash it down, but it wasn't easy and it took several minutes.

What bothers me is that it doesn't act very quickly. In theory, I should be dead by now, but nothing's happened. What if it only works for rats? What a disaster that would be. I'd have no other way but the window. I'd like to have written to Jacques, but there wouldn't have been any point because Mummy would never have given him the letter. I don't suppose he'll even know I'm dead.

Killing yourself has another advantage: the Catholic church doesn't want anything more to do with you, it rejects you. The bore is that you don't get any benefit from this, since you don't exist any more.

I'm really sorry not to have seen *The White Horse Inn*. I know it's normal that Natalie should be the one to go out all the time, since she's the eldest, but things which are normal are seldom very pleasant and there doesn't seem much point in having birthdays if you can't have fun at least on those days.

Dying on my birthday seems very good to me. It's better than dying any old day, just by chance. When Mummy and Natalie are old, they'll die like that, without choosing their time. They won't be able to make a date with their own death, they certainly wouldn't be capable of killing themselves.

In my childhood in the red land I never talked about Natalie, it was as if she never existed. It's a shame she wasn't born into another family. Perhaps if I'd been an only child and she hadn't had a choice, Mummy would have loved me? She might not have realised so clearly that I was a failure? But if Natalie was unwanted in my life, I was certainly an unwanted part of hers. When I'm dead, there will be no need to feed or clothe me, or spend anything on me, and that'll mean more money to buy her dresses.

The good thing about my dying is that it'll make everybody happy.

Apart from Jacques. The only person I love.

But he won't know anything about it.

I feel sleepy. It seems to take ages, waiting to die. I hope it'll be over when Mummy and Natalie get back from Châtelet. I want to die in peace, without getting caught this last time.

I'm going to shut my eyes and go to sleep. It'll come by itself, while I'm asleep. I don't want to think about anyone any more, not even Jacques. Only about the red land.

*

I messed it up, of course. I've never been able to do anything right. Not even die. It must be said that people never let me do what I want. Instead of leaving me to die without bothering me they saved me by force. However much I fought and shouted, 'Let me die,' the doctor who was called out as an emergency, and who lives in the same building as us by the way, made me drink some milk and then vomit, and later, at the hospital, they pumped out my stomach.

But it was my own fault. If I hadn't written to Mummy before I killed myself she wouldn't have come to see what sort of state I was in, when she got back from Châtelet. I wouldn't have been found until I was dead. The rat poison worked very well, after all. Apparently now my stomach is all spoilt and I can no longer eat whatever I want. Doctors are peculiar, though. They talk as if you had a choice. You just eat what you can.

Hospital is a terrifying thing. You feel as if you're in prison, and guilty. There's a doctor whose job is not to look after your body, but the ideas you have in your head, and he came to interrogate me several times. He insisted on knowing why I wanted to kill myself, whether it was because my parents beat me, and everything that happened at home. It reminded me of the priest who seemed so nice and who told on me afterwards. I was sure this doctor would do the same and would tell Mummy everything, so I was suspicious. I was all wilted and crumpled up deep inside myself. I said it was an accident, I hadn't done it on purpose, I was just playing about eating rat poison out of curiosity, to see what effect it'd have, and that I thought it was only harmful to rats. He didn't believe me, that doctor, but since Mummy hadn't shown him the letter he didn't have any proof and in the end he let me off and I was allowed to leave.

In the hospital, Mummy was very nice. So nice that I almost believed she'd started to love me. In front of the nurses and the doctor, she'd say: 'My darling little girl, what came over you? Why did you do it? We love you so much! Thank God I came home in time! Thank God!' She even started to cry. The nurses said to me: 'Your poor Mummy, how could you have done a thing like that to her!' But since I'm so used to being in the wrong, it didn't make the sadness inside me much worse.

Daddy and Natalie didn't come, that's normal, but Mummy was really very good, as if she loved me for real, to such an extent that I was starting to feel better and to tell myself that perhaps we were going to end up being happy together, but I was forgetting she was behaving like that because in front of other people she always behaves as she thinks she ought.

When I left the hospital, she didn't say a single word throughout the ride home. Once we got back to the house, she made me a great speech. I was a monster, a heartless brute, ungrateful, irresponsible, selfish. I thought of no one but myself, I hadn't bothered to consider the consequences of my action. I'd put her in an appalling position, everybody knew what had happened, even the concierge, and what on earth would people think of us now? I was an impossibly difficult child to bring up. They'd paid for my schooling and not one single time had I even managed to come top of the class, yet Natalie often had, and besides there were spelling mistakes in my letter. She had no choice but to put up with me, she would bear her cross to the end, but she would no longer make the efforts she'd made before. If she'd locked me up it was for my own good, and I'd paid her back very badly. Since I was beyond redemption, she'd only bother with me as little as possible. I'd be free to do whatever I wanted, on condition that I kept up appearances and didn't embarrass the family. I must undertake to be on time for meals, and not to go out in the evening or at night, but I'd never be locked up again, I could have a key to the door and during the daytime I could make myself scarce and go wherever I wanted.

At that moment I felt almost mad with happiness. To be free, at last! To be able to go where I wanted, when I wanted, see whoever I liked. To see Jacques again, especially, that was all I could think of. Seeing Jacques again . . . I wonder what would have become of me if Thi Ba had taken me away with her, or my soldier in Hanoi. Would I have been different? Just once, I told Natalie how I missed Thi Ba and Natalie replied that she didn't understand why, Thi Ba was ugly. What does that matter?

Perhaps I'm as ugly as Thi Ba? But beauty depends on your point of view. I can't persuade myself that Natalie is pretty, even though Mummy says she's a great beauty. Besides, Aunt Chloë and Aunt Helene didn't think she was beautiful, but they told me I was very pretty. It's complicated, beauty: nobody agrees about it. The important thing is to like the way you look and Natalie likes the way she looks very much. She's lucky.

She has always been lucky. But she doesn't realise. She finds it quite natural, everything that's done for her. She doesn't see how other people exist, so she can't make any comparison.

It's strange, but I wouldn't like to be Natalie. Even

though she's much better than me. I find that she's missing something important, something that doesn't have a name and which I can't explain. Natalie is not someone you want to take by the hand.

Later on, if I have a safe-house like the one in the red land, the only people who'll come there will be people I want to take by the hand. I shall protect myself. And I'll never be hurt again.

Thoï! That's enough.